# Lights over Bellano

## Robert John Goddard

## ACKNOWLEDGMENTS

Having an idea for a novel and turning it into a cover picture design is hard. I want to thank Andrea for creating a wonderful cover for *Lights over Bellano.*

andrea.price.concept

# PROLOGUE

Kingston-upon-Thames
June 20, 2014

Dear Ms Sands

I would like to resubmit my mother's novel, *Lights over Bellano*, to your agency. You may remember that it concerns a group of English people resident in Italy in the 1980s and how a crime in the town influences their lives. It is similar in theme to other books handled by your agency.

You will recall that my mother submitted the work to you ten years ago. Although you expressed an interest in handling the book at that time, my mother was reluctant to let you do so until certain conditions were met.

With a deft movement of fingers and thumb, Donna Sands flicked the letter over. She did this several times, shaking her head at the blank flipside, before collecting herself and reading on. It was not unusual for the occasional covering letter to make her heart race in excitement. Nor was it unusual for such letters to sadden and disappoint. She was, after all, a leading literary agent and always on the lookout for those introductory lines that impressed her with concise information about the book and its author. The letter she flicked over and over in her hand was unusual in that it prompted excitement and sadness in equal measure. Ten years ago, *Lights over Bellano* was the one that got away, and Bella Norton was the discovered undiscovered talent apparently looking for representation.

Donna stilled her hand, pinched the letter between thumb and forefinger, and focused on the next paragraph.

> As you know, my mother based her story on events that took place, just before her retirement, in the Italian town of *Bellano*. When my mother submitted the manuscript to you in 2004, many of the people, on whom the characters in her story were based, were still alive. My mother did not want to offend anyone who might feel misrepresented in some way.

Donna slid the letter onto her desk and sat back in her swivel chair. She rested her chin on steepled fingers and scrutinized the manuscript. It was divided into four rectangles by a criss-cross of rubber bands but the name of the author and the title stood out in the top right-hand corner: *Lights over Bellano by Bella Norton*.

Donna shook her head. Had ten years really passed since she slipped this novel from the slush pile? In 2004, she had just started out in her career in books. Ambitious and eager to prove herself, she read everything that was sent to her. Nonetheless, few synopses impressed in the way that Bella Norton's did. It was well-structured, informative and clear about the book's themes of roots and home. Furthermore, the first page of the manuscript contained no errors, the grammar was faultless and it grabbed her attention. Once she had started reading the novel, she could not put it down. When she did put it down, she knew that with careful editing and a few changes it would be a winner. It literally held her by the collar and said: "Take me on."

But, for the first and last time in Donna's career, a writer declined the offer of representation. Despite Donna's best efforts, she was unable to persuade the old lady that demand for European crime fiction was high and that she had written a potential best seller. Bella was adamant. She refused to have the book published until "a certain time" had passed.

Donna reached out for the letter again.

> You know that my mother passed away in 2008 but she asked me to resubmit the manuscript should the major players in the *Bellano* case die before me. I can now confirm that Ralph Connor and his wife were recently killed in a car crash on the hills overlooking *Bellano*. They were on their way back from a hilltop restaurant called *La Casa Rossa* when the car – a 1989 Lancia Delta – left the road, crashed down a hillside and burst into flames. They would have been killed instantly. Ralph was 64 years old, his wife 62. My sources tell me that these two were very happy together and inseparable. It is, perhaps, fitting that they died together. I am also told that the school has since been bought by Archie and Catriona McKenzie. Both have brought

originality and a dynamism that the school needed to survive.

With regard to other players, Nick Radcliffe has been dead for over ten years – murdered on his way home one evening while working with the British Council in Bangkok. With regard to Francesca, she was diagnosed with borderline personality disorder soon after the incidents described in the book. She was committed to a care home in 1992. I am told that it is unlikely that she will ever be allowed back into the community. Consequently, I can now fulfill my mother's wishes and send you the manuscript, which you are now free to handle.

Donna let the page drop into her lap. She was reminded of her fondness for the old lady. Donna had even taken advantage of a trip to the Italian Riviera in 2006 to visit the town of *Bellano* where Bella had lived. Bella had arrived there by accident, aged twenty-six, in 1946 while on her way to Florence. But she fell in love and stayed in Italy until 1995. She never did visit Florence but she did revive and run *Bellano*'s English-language library. When Donna visited it, the library still opened its doors three afternoons a week. There were rows and rows of faded spines providing a snapshot of what had appealed to readers in the forties, fifties and sixties. Some of the authors remained familiar but it was clear from the dust they had collected that most books remained untouched. Donna allowed her memory to linger a while longer on the library's shelves while she fumbled for the page in her lap.

I am also enclosing a letter from my

mother. It was her wish that I pass this on to you with the resubmitted manuscript.

Thank you again for reading the work. Please feel free to call me at home if you need to discuss anything.

Yours sincerely
Ivy Norton (daughter)

Donna leaned forward and picked up the manuscript with both hands. She lifted it to her face, closed her eyes and smelled the pages as if their odour might halt the slide away from memories of her trip to *Bellano*. She examined the manuscript from a variety of angles. A small envelope – a letter from beyond the grave - was pinned on the corner. FAO Donna Sands was written across it.

Donna sighed. The publishing industry was not static like the English library in *Bellano*. Few people in the 21$^{st}$ century read its books by Cecil Roberts, Ernest Raymond or G A Henty. Furthermore, this process was accelerating. What was popular in 2004 might not work in 2014. Most importantly, if Bella had based her story on actual events, it may not be enough that the major players were dead. There was a real risk of libel.

Donna also knew that a literary agent's job was not for the indecisive or the hesitant. She glanced at her watch. She would give this manuscript no more attention than she would any other. She poured herself another coffee and started reading.

# 1

It was 16.29. Ralph was on his feet and fumbling in the overhead racks when the distortions of a Tannoy system announced his imminent arrival on platform seven. Ralph glanced through the window as the platform sped into view, and the voice of a station official crackled through the speakers.

*"Bellano Centrale. Bellano Centrale."*

The train was some minutes behind time but Francesca would not accept this as an excuse for his being late.

"Five o'clock," she had said. Leaning forward, she had raised her hand to her ear and let it hover for a second before hissing, "Sharp."

She had brought her hand down guillotine-like on his desk, and Ralph still heard his coffee cup rattling in response while he secured his rucksack to his back, pushed through the corridor and opened the train door. Flitting in and out of eyeshot, hands grabbed at luggage, eyes watched and platform vendors jostled. Ralph did not wait for the train to come to a complete standstill before alighting. On this afternoon his feet were on the platform and striding for the exit while the brakes were at shrieking pitch and Francesca's voice was ringing in his ears.

"Don't be late."

He usually stopped for a glass of wine in the station bar. He enjoyed the nonconformity of this place where the town's underbelly rubbed shoulders with the smug and well-to-do. But that afternoon, he strode through the transvestites, the pick-ups, the pimps and assorted other undesirables and barged his way into the ticket hall. Heading for the exit doors, Ralph saw Francesca's finger wagging in his mind's eye. His right hand rose of its own accord and brushed the spot on his forearm that she had found, fingered and squeezed.

Leaning into the station doors, Ralph made a slight shake of the head to shift his fringe from his eyes. He emerged in the taxi area and caught his breath. Freezing air gripped his ears and cheeks and a blur around the street lamps suggested that fog was coming down. He saw it in the exhaust fumes, watched it hovering in the yellowed lights over the railway tracks. January fog was common in the Plain of the *Po*. In *Bellano*, it could last for days.

Ralph shivered and rubbed at his ear lobes before hunching into his coat and pulling up its collar. He scanned the rows of cars grabbing the limelight under car-park flood lamps. The sight of his Alfa Romeo GT brought a gleam to his eyes and he strode towards it, reaching in his pocket for the ignition key while several cars circled round him, their headlamps turned off while they looked for pickings. Ralph had checked the bumpers of his vehicle and was running his hands over its restored bodywork when one of the circling cars squeaked to a halt beside him. A window slid down and a voice from the passenger seat mumbled an offer. Ralph turned away, threw his rucksack into the boot of his car and slammed the lid down. Just shy of forty, Ralph did not like having his privacy invaded. He expected others to respect his life choices and allow him to get on with them at his own pace. The car was unimpressed by Ralph's likes and expectations. It stood there throbbing and refusing to move while cigarette smoke billowed through the window, and a leather-gloved hand rubbed the gear knob.

Ralph slipped into his car, inserted the ignition key and slanted his eyes upwards to the rear-view mirror. The other vehicle was whispering away into the cover of nightfall but a glimpse of the number plate told Ralph that the circling car was from out of town. Still looking into the mirror, Ralph refocused and found his own eyes. Their expression confirmed what the tightened lips and pale skin already told him. Dropping his eyelids, Ralph took a deep breath to ease the anger these scavengers provoked. And their pickings, the human beings, male or female, were visible just a few metres from him. Propped up against trees they were offering their bodies for the next shot of heroin.

"Bastards," Ralph said.

He turned the key and the Alfa sprang into life. He let the engine idle for a few moments, enjoying its familiar pitch, before pulling away from temptation and into the traffic on the town ring. He glanced at his watch and headed for the city walls. They were visible in the middle distance as a seasonal glow of neon lights decorating the ramparts with the greeting, "Welcome to 1989." They were already four days into the new year and the number "8" was leaning sideways and flickering its way to an early death.

Ralph had known Francesca since he helped to found The Conrad School of Languages in the late seventies.

The word "languages" – in the plural – was a misnomer. The school taught one language – English - and, ten years on, Francesca's English was fluent. But she usually enrolled on one of the school's language-related programmes and had already completed the advanced grammar course with Paul Loban, English Literature 1 with Miss O'Henry and English Crime Novels with Mrs Norton. Until recently, Francesca had been as familiar in the school as the secretary, Maria Teresa. So familiar was she that Ralph had not found it odd to have a drink with her one warm summer night the previous year. They had discussed Francesca's current language needs and considered her future options. Afterwards, they had strolled through *Piazza Dante* with the light of the moon and with stray and distant cries following them through the shadows of the porticos. Francesca had even been inspired to tell him about the love of her life.

Ralph changed down and roared through the curve that led into the *Piazza Del Risorgimento*. The tyres, squealing on the cobblestones, pleased him. The fog was thickening over the street lamps. He flicked at the windscreen wash and the wipers responded with a swish that brought him a clear but transient view of the memorial that dominated the square. His thoughts touched on the 2000 deaths it commemorated before the monument disappeared in a smear of grit and moisture. When the wipers swished again, Ralph was past the square and heading for the old town.

Francesca had told him that the love of her life was the most handsome and intriguing man she had ever seen. Tall and fair, but with a hint of world-weary danger, he was, she insisted, a cross between a 19th-century poet and a Hollywood star. The minute she spotted him in the school, she knew she had to have him. Instantly, she was madly in love. The big problem, she added, looking right into Ralph's eyes, was drawing herself to his attention.

Ralph decelerated through the medieval town gate and crawled towards *Viale Porta Nuova*. The avenue was so brightly lit that the world around it was invisible. It was lined on both sides with wide and glistening marble pavements. Reflected in them, the fashionable shop fronts and paper-chains of coloured Christmas lights lay like some separate underworld. Whole families in identical green coats, strolled and chatted between these two worlds and occasionally disappeared through shop doorways, lured away by their brighter lights and promises.

Approaching *Piazza Cavour*, Ralph thought that he had made all the right noises that evening with Francesca. And when she paused, he was ready with the right kind of question. Was the tall and fair-haired man married? Had he shown any interest in her? Ralph was about to voice these questions when they were approached by two young people, probably addicts, asking for money. Ralph allowed Francesca to slip her arm in his and he led her to one side of them. By the time they reached his car, her arm remained stubbornly hooked in his but the intimate tone of their conversation had been beyond recapture.

That summer night in *Piazza Dante* was five months away from this foggy evening but he recalled the passion expressed by her voice. It was not at odds with the fiery voice which had demanded an appointment – it was simply at different ends of the same scale. Nonetheless, the presence in her tone of another emotion had stayed in his ears and disturbed his weekend in London. It was the novelty that struck him. Francesca was passionate and communicative but Ralph had never before heard her express fear.

It was 16.52 when Ralph arrived in the vicinity of the school. He spotted a parking space on the corner of *Via*

*Tommaso da Modena* and *Via Vittorio Veneto*, reversed into it and switched off the car lamps. He remained seated, enjoying the sound of the engine while he watched the fog dropping to street level and moisture settling on the windscreen. When it eventually dispersed, the fog would leave its heart behind as a coating of dust and grit on the exposed surfaces of the town.

Ralph switched on the intermittent wiper control. The school entrance was a stone's throw away but he saw the outline of the brushed metal sign stamped on the entrance door. Its text read: "Conrad School of Languages" and the colour logo showed a ship in full sail. The logo had been the idea of Ralph's colleague Nick. The symbol told the world that the passport to international travel was the English language.

The wiper swished back and forth, and Ralph spotted Nick's silhouette framed on the blinds of a first-floor classroom window. For a moment, Nick was still and holding his hands in front of him as though in the process of taking holy communion. Rising slowly, Nick's shadow assumed the shape of some gothic monster about to commit a dreadful act. He guessed Nick was supervising one of his role-plays, simulations or case studies. Most of the other teachers had expressed doubts about Discovery Learning when Nick had suggested adopting its techniques some years previously. The belief that something discovered would be more meaningful and memorable than something simply presented had not met with a positive response from Ralph either. What was worse, he and Nick had hardly been able to confine their antagonism to teaching methodology. Personal differences had emerged – differences in background, class, and regional attitudes. Ralph now admitted that Nick's perseverance had eventually paid off. Discovery Learning was becoming increasingly popular amongst young business people. It was also very lucrative.

Ralph watched and considered Nick until the moisture on the windscreen blocked him from view and a farting sound alerted Ralph to the fact that his wipers were sticking to the glass. Making a mental note to change them, Ralph flicked off the wiper switch, turned off the engine and removed the car key. He got out of the car and locked it. Facing him, a large knot of students was gathered by the entrance door. Their number reinforced his view that, for many of them, his school had become nothing more than a central hub, along with the *piazza* and the bars, for information gathering and dispersal. On the edge of this knot, a cluster of yellow and blue scarves marked the presence of supporters of the town's football club.

Ralph was threading his way through the blue and yellow group when he jumped at a drum beat, a rat-a-tat-tat in his ear. He swung round at the roar of laughter which followed but the drummer had backed away. A number of the group crowded round him and placated him with "*Ciao Ralph, tutto bene*?" The words were accompanied by the touch of hands on his upper arms and shoulders. The hands did not linger. They never did. They touched him as recognition of his presence and they flickered away, the fingers brushing his arm like tentacles. He did not see Francesca's brother, Piero, but Ralph had sensed the power of his presence, had heard the roar of his laughter – always the loudest, always the longest.

Ralph jostled through a crowd of students descending the stairs. He lowered his eyes. They settled on the sensible black shoes and solid calves of the school secretary, Maria Teresa, making her way home. Her discreet "Good evening," was followed by a short silence and then: "Welcome back. How was merry England?"

But she was too far down the stairs for him to tell her that he had expected to be greeted by friendly policemen, nice old ladies, red double-decker buses lining the road and red post-boxes standing on each and every street corner. Instead he had been shocked to hear the thwack of a mother's hand on a little girl's legs and a raucous shout, "Shut up yer fuckin' little bleeder." The memory of it still haunted him.

Ralph arrived in the school lobby as the last of the students bustled out of the school and the contract cleaners picked up broom and mop to prepare the premises for the following day. Glancing to his right, he saw that the door to his office was open. Sitting at his desk with her profile to him, Francesca was waiting. She was staring at the floor, her long black hair falling forward curtain-like over her face. Perhaps sensing his presence, she swept her hair behind her right ear and swivelled her head towards him, her eyebrow raised like a question mark on her forehead.

Ralph heard the last of the teachers hurrying down the stairs. Apart from the cleaners, he and Francesca were alone in the school. Ralph stepped into his office and closed the door behind him.

## 2

He wondered whether it had been a noise from the
street below that woke him from another bad
dream. Ralph glanced at his bedside clock and dragged
the blanket up to his chin. He lay still and chased the tail
of his nightmare but he could not say whether the noise
he had heard belonged to the nightmare or to the real
world. The sounds, which were drifting into his bedroom
from the streets below, told him that the fog was still
down. It absorbed or scattered the heartbeat of the town.
Conversations seemed whispered; car engines were
muted. Only low-pitched tones seemed to survive the
fog and they lent a bass rhythm to the passage of the
morning. Perhaps it was this rhythm that had woken
him.

A distant clinking of glass or china ceramic made
him blink. The sound suggested that the corner bar was
open. In his mind's eye, Ralph watched the *barista*,
Giuseppe. He was serving coffee and *grappa* to the
workmen digging up the cobblestones near the town
gate. When Ralph's thoughts veered off to take stock of
the previous evening, he shook his head, swung his feet

to the floor and reached for the portable radio. Francesca's allegations had haunted him for most of the night. The words "stalker" and "scandal" had even appeared in his dreams. Freed from any restraints, they had ridden roughshod and created a variety of nightmare scenarios. Most of these had ended with scandal, the closure of the school and redundant teachers.

He switched on the radio and tuned in to the local station. It was 8 o'clock and the newsreader was reporting that the airport was closed due to fog, and there were speed restrictions on the motorways. Ralph strode into the bathroom and fumbled for his razor. He was splashing his face with water when the newsreader mentioned the wealthy *Bellano* suburb of *Montebelluna*. Ralph pushed himself upright and turned his dripping face towards the radio. Apparently, the police had been called out to deal with some sort of disturbance in *Montebelluna* during the night.

He hurried into his bedroom, dressed at a rush and threw open the curtains. Making for the kitchen, he was intending to greet the day with a smile but dreariness from the world outside prompted barely more than a grin. He made a coffee, slumped at the kitchen table and fingered his fringe away from his eyes. He continued to rub his forehead with his fingertips while thoughts about his recent interview in London provided him with a useful distraction. The Director of the Central London School, Dr Banks, had seemed to like him. If Ralph were offered the job, he might take it as a lifeline and get out of Italy while he could.

Looking through the windows for advice, Ralph found only fog and water droplets on the panes. Both made him feel insecure, unsure of what he should do next. He opened his notepad and wrote down initial ideas for his agenda for the morning staff meeting. There were staffing issues at Ederle, the cake maker, and with

NATO HQ. There were also encouraging noises from Hoskins the chemicals company and Ralph had been invited back to give a second presentation. He fingered the pencil and wrote: "Hire more teachers?"

He twiddled the pencil between his fingers, tapped it on his bottom teeth and told himself that he should be facing his priorities and considering his response to Francesca's allegations. Dealing with the personal and emotional issues she had mentioned were not things he counted as being among his strengths. He dealt with potential and actual clients, represented the school, and handled the bank and other financial issues. He loved following up leads and thrilled in the hunt for more customers but he was unsure about how to react to suggestions of deviant and obsessive behaviour in a colleague and friend.

He would have to confront Nick with Francesca's complaints but Ralph needed to come across as non-accusatory and he doubted his ability to hide his resentment that the school's reputation and their livelihood might be compromised should Nick's alleged behaviour come to light. He considered mentioning the problem to Nick in passing, almost as an afterthought. Ralph imagined himself uttering the words "stalker" and "scandal" as an afterthought and dismissed the idea immediately. However he managed to dress up the words, the results might be the same. Nick would feel that Ralph was victimising him. Denial and increased hostility towards Ralph would follow.

Ralph tore out the agenda, put his notebook and pencil aside and reached for his Hoskins presentation slides. He made his second coffee to the sound of the 9 o'clock news broadcast. The airport would remain shut for some days, the news reader reported, and the disturbance in *Montebelluna* had developed into an incident that required a substantial police presence and an ambulance. Ralph cut the reader off by bringing the palm of his hand down hard on the off switch. He allowed his hand to hover over it as though the radio might take on a life of its own and cough back into life. He snatched his hand away when he saw it trembling, placed it in his lap and calmed it by burying its knuckle in the palm of his other hand. He sat like that for several minutes and reflected on the possible repercussions of the previous evening. Eventually, he slipped the agenda into his jacket pocket, closed the door to his flat and stepped across the corridor to the school.

Those incoming students gathered in the entrance hall were in animated conversational competition with the outgoing students. From below, shouts funnelled up the stairwell and burst through the entrance door.

"Down with foreigners."

"*Viva Italia.*"

Ralph stood on the school threshold, breathing hard and reflecting that good-natured banter was common after international football matches. This particular banter had an edge to it which suggested that an Italian team had lost unfairly the previous evening. Questions about which teams had been playing were overlaid by returning concerns about the evening before. Ralph decided to banish these by estimating the value of the clothes and accessories that were displayed by students in the entrance hall. He reckoned that the fur coats and the jewellery alone represented a small fortune. Their owners were conversing simultaneously and the talk was accompanied by gestures that rattled bracelets and punctuated verbal expressions. Ralph spotted Stefano, the genial but two-faced journalist from the regional paper. He was standing in the doorway of Ralph's office and Ralph set off towards him. He weaved his way through the large and central knot of fur, jewellery and fingernails so long that they reminded him of red baguettes. He flicked his fringe, smiled his boyish smile at these wives and daughters of *Bellano*'s great and good and shelved the fact that, for most of them, studying English was merely a fashion statement. He knew that were a sex scandal to come to light, the students would look elsewhere for their English language accessories. From the babble of voices came another voice.

"Eh, Ralph. *Cosa ne sai tu*? What do you know about it all?"

Ralph turned his head. Most students talked to him formally using *lei* - the polite Italian form of the English word "you". The informal *tu* was disrespectful and everyone knew it. Its use temporarily silenced the gathering in the entrance hall.

Deciding to ignore the provocation, Ralph pushed and smiled his way to his office door but Stefano had sidled away and joined Danilo against the wall. Danilo was one of the school's success stories. He had fallen in love with his non-Italian-speaking teacher, Evelyn, and after four months he had reached a good intermediate level of English. Unfortunately for The Conrad School, Ralph thought, love alone would not keep the business afloat. From the bottom of the stairs came another shout:

"It must be German pricks."

"Or the English, eh Ralph? We – the Italians - are not capable of such terrible things."

Danilo seemed on the point of making an angry response but Stefano laid a restraining hand on his shoulder and muttered something in his ear. The school secretary, Maria Teresa, came to the rescue with smiles for everybody and pretended to embrace them all while she rounded up the students and herded them towards the classrooms. When they had chattered their way through their classroom doors, Maria Teresa turned to Ralph and rubbed the palms of her hands together as though relishing the situation.

"They are excited," she said with a slight shrug. "It is just rumours."

Ralph shook his head.

"About?"

Maria Teresa stepped behind him and took a seat at her desk outside his office door. She cocked her head and studied him for some time before commenting:

"You must eat more, Ralph. You aren't looking after yourself."

"I'm fine. So, what are...?"

"Only you look as white as a sheet. You need more sleep, you know?"

"Really, I'm OK."

"You're not OK."

Maria Teresa leaned forward and raised a wagging finger. She then waved her hands in front of her and proceeded to lecture him on the dangers of stress and heart disease. She ended with arms wide open and made the predictable appeal.

"You must find a woman, settle down and have children."

Maria Teresa had been urging him to settle down ever since that momentous day at the beginning of the 1978-79 school year when he, Nick and Louise had rebelled against their erstwhile employer, the ELS School of English. As the ELS School's secretary, Maria Teresa had been taking the minutes at the staff meeting for the school's owner, *Signora* Compri. Sitting in a bright red outfit and adjusting the position of a chunky gold bracelet on her wrist, *Signora* Compri had refused to up wages and conditions before demanding maximum availability, maximum flexibility and maximum professionalism. Shifting her bottom in her large leather armchair, she paused to let the message sink in.

"Any questions?" she had asked.

A few young teachers with hangovers made

mumblings of dissent, but Ralph, Nick and Louise resigned at the end of the week and Maria Teresa had resigned with them. She had been mothering them ever since.

"What are these rumours you mention, Maria Teresa?"

"*Montebelluna*, of course," she said.

"You've lost me," Ralph said.

"The man who died," she said. "Rumour has it he was murdered. They say it was foreigners."

Ralph licked his lips and swallowed down a lump of streaky saliva.

"Someone died?"

"Murdered," Maria Teresa said. "Murdered by foreigners. That's what the rumours say."

She pushed back her chair, walked round the table and grabbed Ralph's elbow.

"Are you sure you are alright, Ralph? You really are as white as a sheet."

Ralph felt his nostrils twitch and his face went cold. He counted to three before saying:

"Maybe the criminals are locals, Maria Teresa. Remember what happened a few months ago?"

Ralph's comment silenced Maria Teresa, and she and Ralph stared into each other's eyes - remembering. The previous autumn an elderly man shot his son dead out of exasperation at his demands for money to buy heroin. A little later, a sixteen-year-old girl shot her father dead, accusing him of repeated sexual abuse. Nobody could believe that these crimes were home-grown.

Maria Teresa lifted her shoulders and emitted an abbreviated vowel sound from her throat.

"You asked me," she said, "and that's what the rumours say. And you need some rest. You look terrible."

Ralph said nothing more. He knew that rumours in

Italy had an accuracy he had never known back home in England. Information flowed quickly through vast networks of personal contacts. What Ralph once saw as messy and inefficient, he now saw as effective in the context of Italian life. Hints and suggestions took precedence over facts, and listeners were expected to make the relevant connections.

"By the way," said Maria Teresa, looking up from some papers that lay across her desk. "Louise is in the bar downstairs. She asked me to tell you."

"Does she want to speak to me?"

Maria Teresa rolled her eyes and picked up the phone book.

"Do I have to spell it out?"

Ralph hovered at the desk, holding his hands in a gesture of surrender.

"Is there anything else I can help you with, Ralph?"

He shook his head, spun round and strode through the door. Maria Teresa's entreaties to get a good meal followed him down the stairs but students were already streaming up the other way in numbers which both drowned her out and brought a smile of contentment to Ralph's face. The numbers were a testament to the success of his hard work.

Ten years previously, neither he nor Nick or Louise had known that their decision to set up a new school coincided with a nationwide boom in the demand for English language learning. The numbers of students enrolled at the school had outstripped their wildest dreams. It turned out that they all played a part in their success. Ralph was an excellent salesperson and Nick was the great theorist and always willing to try out cutting edge methodologies in the classroom. Louise was made of different stuff.

Wrapping his arms around himself, Ralph bustled through the building entrance and hurried along the street. He paused when he reached the corner opposite the bar. Through the fog, the bar had lost its substance, and Giuseppe, standing at the battery of levers that made up his coffee machine, looked like a ghostly apparition. Ralph crossed the street and stopped just short of the glass window.

Louise's presence was signalled by her coat and bag, which lay discarded on a chair by the door. The casual dismissal of these items was a deliberate slap in the face for the fashionable and a statement of her own individuality. Louise herself was present in the warm glow that emanated from the long red hair tumbling over her shoulders and down her back. She seemed oblivious to the workmen staring at her from around the edges of the bar.

Ralph hesitated a moment longer. Telling Louise about Francesca's accusations would give them a reality that could not be ignored. He also knew he was going to omit some details and this, he knew, was tantamount to lying and an admission of his own responsibilities. He placed his hand on the door and pushed it open.

# 3

A gust of freezing air accompanied Ralph through the glass door and rushed into the bar to catch a strand of Louise's red hair. She tucked it behind her ear and, without turning, she said:

"They say that your thirties are your best years."

Ralph stood with a hand on the door while tongues of fog curled into the bottom of his trousers and licked up his leg. He remained still but allowed his eyes to sweep over every nook and cranny in the bar. The workmen were gathering themselves but there was nobody else in sight. The coffee machine hissed, but the *barista*, Giuseppe, was nowhere to be seen.

Louise tilted her chin upwards and shook her head so that her red locks shifted down her back.

"At thirty-something, you're supposed to finally have a handle on your relationships. You're supposed to have a respectable collection of shoes and you're supposed to be on track at work. In other words, you're supposed to have got your act together."

Ralph's mind raced to find an explanation for this soliloquy. Perhaps she was learning some presentation by heart. Maybe, some bad news had arrived and sent her over the edge of sanity. Ralph doubted it. He had known few people as grounded as Louise. He saw this composure now in the way she was standing at the bar, feet apart, balanced and steady, and dismissive of the ogling workmen around her. Ralph was also confident that, had she been confronted with bad news, she would have told him. Exchanging confidences over a bottle of wine in some shaded *piazza* had defined their relationship since their first meeting in the autumn of 1976. Fresh from her course in Criminal Law, Louise had been sitting in the staffroom of the ELS School and, Ralph recalled, wore her personality over her head like a halo. First conversations with Louise confirmed Ralph's initial perceptions of intelligence and goodness. She had become unenthusiastic about criminal law. The prospect of a life dealing with human unhappiness was no longer appealing and she had come to Italy to think her life through.

"I'm watching you, Ralph," she said. "There's no need to look at me as if I'd got *delirium tremens*."

Ralph shifted his gaze to the mirror behind the bar. Louise would have seen him coming long before he touched the door.

"So, my relationship with Tiziano's going wrong but two out of three ain't bad, is it? We are still together."

A questioning intonation hung between them with the currents of cold air and the tramping feet of the workmen.

"*Ciao, ciao*," they said pulling their coats around them and clumping towards the door. Ralph stepped sideways. The currents of cold air became a shiver-producing gale when the door swung open and the men filed out and into the fog. Ralph shook himself and rubbed at his hands.

"Still?" he said.

"Yes, still."

Ralph raised his hands to his mouth and blew on them. He had once discussed the meaning of the word "still" with Paul Loban, the grammar guru. They had come to the conclusion that "still" implied that time was running out.

"I'm sorry to hear that," Ralph said to the floor. But he knew her too well to expect her to accept his condolences without comment.

"You have to accept things as they are," Louise said. "Being sorry will change nothing."

Ralph wanted to give Louise his usual lecture on the advantages of taking action and the disadvantages of doing nothing when he was distracted by a group of fog-shadows gathered under the street lamp on the corner opposite. Ralph screwed up his eyes and pushed his head forward but he was unable to identify any of them.

"On the house," said a voice.

Giuseppe had jumped up from behind the counter. He was holding a bottle of *prosecco* in one hand and smiling broadly. As if by magic, he plucked two glasses from behind the bar, lifted them into the air and brought them down on the counter.

Ralph took another look at the shadows in the street. He guessed they were students gathering for a chat before their lessons but their faceless presence was unsettling. He thought he knew them but without the reassurance of sight or sound he was now unsure. At that moment, they were silhouettes looking in his direction.

A hissing pop from the bar made Ralph turn. Giuseppe's was holding the bottle into his groin, while the cork slid into the palm of his other hand. He was folding a towel around the neck of the bottle when Louise did a half pirouette and extended her arms in a gesture of welcome. Ralph stepped towards her, placed one hand on her elbow and the other hand on her opposite shoulder, searched her eyes and kissed her cheek.

Louise pulled away and watched Giuseppe polishing the glasses with a dish towel. He placed them on the counter and, one by one, he tilted the glasses and filled them. When he had finished, he twisted the bottle and lifted it into the air.

"*Salute*," Giuseppe said.

"Cheers," said Ralph and Louise in unison.

Louise put down her glass, looked sideways at Ralph and said:

"Available evidence suggests that Anglo-Italian relationships seldom work."

A bead of wine was glistening on Louise's lower lip. Ralph turned his head when she licked it away.

"Imagine someone came to you and said, 'So, Ralph, I'll have a relationship with you but I shall apply conditions. Essentially, you have to be like me. That means, you eat like me, think like me and share my values,'..." Louise raised her hand to silence any objections before challenging him with, "What would you say to such an offer?"

Ralph barely heard her. He was listening to hammering from the street. He supposed the workmen had started again on the cobblestones. The shapes under the streetlamp appeared to be growing and shifting. But he heard no sound from them. The fog was challenging everything he had taken for granted. It obscured the familiar and the banal. He had been in this bar with Louise on many occasions. Everything was still in the same place, but now it was somehow distorted.

"Hello, Ralph? Are you there? You look like you saw a ghost."

"I need to tell you something," Ralph said.

Ralph hesitated and glanced through the bar's glass frontage. The fog showed no signs of thinning.

Occasionally, hunched and dark figures with hands clutching at the lapels of their coats strode away from the group under the street lamp. He was still watching when two of these hunched figures bundled into the bar with another blast of cold and humid air. The new arrivals unwrapped themselves from hats and scarves and rubbed their hands together. Ralph recognised them as two students but he was somehow detached from them and he saw them now as the enemy, along with the fog and along with the cold.

"I came to see you last night," Louise said.

Ralph froze. At that moment, Louise was a shape in his peripheral vision, the corners of her mouth hidden behind the curling red hair.

"You seemed to be busy," she said.

Ralph inhaled and held his breath while, from somewhere in the town, a peeling of church bells rolled towards the bar. Their tone was deep and resonant and sounded like a death knell, but Ralph was glad of the bells. Their familiarity pleased him. It was also easier to remain silent. He felt that words of excuse or explanation might shift his friendship with Louise to another place.

"I wanted to ask you how the interview went," Louise said.

Ralph exhaled and launched into his response with enthusiasm. Louise shook her head in disbelief when he told her that the interview panel showed no interest in his accomplishments in Italy, and she laughed when Ralph told her how one panellist asked why he wanted to give up the land of sunshine, sports cars, opera and beautiful girls and come back to rainy London.

"They and you are clearly living in different worlds," Louise said.

She searched for his eyes but Ralph head was turned, his eyes staring at the growing number of shapes under the street lamp. He reached out and made to touch her hand with his. He stopped just short of skin contact.

"Just a moment," he said. "I've got something to say to you."

Louise watched him and cocked her head sideways.

"Come on, Ralph. Spit it out."

"Nick."

"Nick?"

"Yes Nick. We've had a complaint."

Louise stood stock still.

"About?"

"Francesca came to see me," he said to his feet.

Louise turned her head sideways as if she had been slapped.

"Oh, yes?"

During the night, in the open-eyed moments, Ralph had tried to remember whether Francesca had used the word "stalker" or whether it was a later invention of his own. But her fear had been real and present in her voice and in her big brown eyes. Ralph recalled the warmth and pressure of Francesca's hand on his forearm. It had lingered there a few moments longer than comfort allowed but Ralph told himself that, perhaps, the hand had been searching for reassurance and security. When he pushed back his chair and stood up, Francesca had been staring up at him with her hand hanging empty over the table. Ralph decided not to mention the hand to Louise.

"She told me she was being stalked."

"By whom?"

"By Nick?"

He had not intended to add the questioning intonation but he needed to hear her say, 'No, it is not possible,' but Louise remained both silent and still for some time. Then, she tossed her head and allowed her hair to settle like a wig over her shoulders.

"Can she produce evidence?"

Her voice was calm and matter-of-fact.

"At first, she thought it was coincidence," Ralph said. "She often bumped into him in the evening. Then, these meetings started happening regularly."

"So – what exactly did she want from you?"

"She wants me to talk to him."

"So, you haven't spoken to him yet?"

"Not yet."

"Why not?"

"Because I haven't seen him."

"Has she been to the police?"

Ralph shook his head and watched his shuffling feet.

"Apparently," he said, "Nick is hanging around outside her house."

"Are there any witnesses?"

Ralph shook his head again.

"She is really frightened – so frightened she would not go home yesterday."

"Do we have any suggestions of personal complications with Nick?"

"And she's looking for revenge? I don't think so. She says she doesn't want to go to the police but..."

Louise blinked.

"OK. We have to act now. We can't afford a re-run of the Mercer scandal."

Ralph nodded. Several years previously, the local and national press had had a field day when a fifteen-year-old girl had run off with John Mercer, her thirty-year-old English teacher working at one of the smaller schools in *Bellano*. The pair absconded the day after police questioned the teacher about the relationship. The couple took a train to Florence with the teenager using the teacher's wife's passport.

This sparked off an intensive search and the man was arrested in Bologna several days later. At the trial which followed, the chief prosecutor argued that although the girl had gone willingly to Bologna, Mr Mercer could not use this as a defence. Mr Mercer had committed a gross and long-term breach of trust. This was not Romeo and Juliet, he said, but a fifteen-year-old girl and a thirty-year-old teacher. Furthermore, when parents send their children to school, they properly expect that those who teach their children will behave in an appropriate manner.

There followed a debate in the press about private language schools in general and private English language schools in particular. Was anyone guaranteeing quality? Were there sexual predators masquerading as professional teachers? The debate rumbled on until football-match-fixing allegations replaced it.

The John Mercer scandal had led to the closure or slimming down of several language schools in *Bellano*. This had been followed by redundancies and a pool of unemployed teaching talent. This talent included highly experienced older teachers. With the help of Louise's judgement, they had been able to select the best of the best and The Conrad School snapped them up.

"I'll speak to Nick immediately after the meeting," Louise said, picking up her mohair coast and throwing it over her shoulders. Ralph watched her slide her hands into the sleeves. Their eyes briefly met and moved away when she arched her back and angled her head to allow her hair to fall free.

"You know," Ralph said, "I really shouldn't come out without a coat. I'll catch my death."

She grabbed his arm and pulled him towards her as they walked out into the fog. Ralph allowed Louise to lead him back to the school. He heard nothing from the group under the street lamp and he hardly recognised the street he was walking along. He felt his way with his feet and found it unfamiliar and uneven.

When they arrived in the school's entrance hall, a wide-eyed Maria Teresa sprang up from her desk and barred their way to the classrooms.

"The crime in *Montebelluna*," she said.

Ralph felt Louise slip her arm into his and grip it.

"A tragedy," Maria Teresa said. "Such a fine man and an example to all of us."

Louise tightened her grip on Ralph's arm and shook her head to suggest ignorance. Maria Teresa widened her eyes still further and opened her arms in amazement.

"Why, *Signor* Merighi, of course," she said.

"The architect," Ralph whispered almost to himself.

Maria Teresa nodded.

"Not any architect," she said, "but the man who masterminded the reconstruction of *Bellano* in the late fifties and sixties."

Maria Teresa closed her arms and grasped Ralph's free arm with both hands.

"You are not alright, Ralph. Only I have always told you never to go out in the fog without a coat."

"I'm fine," Ralph said.

"You're not fine. You look like you're going down with something."

Then she turned to Louise and said:

"He needs a good woman to look after him."

"Please get to the point, Maria Teresa," Ralph said.

"*Signor* Merighi will forever live in the rows of houses and the blocks of flats that stand now on the area by the station. The composition of roads, pedestrian pathways, *piazzas* and green areas were his hallmark and..."

"Please, Maria Teresa. What has happened?"

"He was on his way home from a prayer meeting and someone was lying in wait for him with a metal bar. He was bludgeoned to death. His own son, Piero, discovered the body early this morning."

Louise lifted her hands to her face and covered her mouth.

"They say he was beaten beyond recognition," Maria Teresa said.

"Metal bar?" Ralph said. "What metal bar?"

But Maria Teresa was not to be interrupted.

"Poor Piero," Maria Teresa said. "And his poor sister Francesca. It must be terrible for them."

"Yes, of course," Louise said. She tipped her head sideways and tucked another unruly strand of red hair behind her ear. "Francesca and her brother Piero were amongst our first students, weren't they, Ralph?"

But she was talking to the air. Ralph had dropped into a chair beside her.

# 4

They were ready and waiting for him behind the door. While his fingers fumbled for the doorknob, Ralph heard their voices. Their tone suggested that the room he was about to enter was stirring with discontent. Louise put a restraining hand on his forearm as they entered the room.

"Calm down, Ralph," she whispered, "and give them a break."

The swell of voices ebbed when Ralph and Louise took their seats. Ralph crossed his legs and noted that nobody was looking in his direction. Scanning the faces in front of him, Ralph saw that the older teachers, picked up in the fallout from the Mercer scandal, were ignoring everyone by conversing amongst themselves in a tight group. The youngsters seemed to be suffering from varying degrees of hangover. They were scattered and disorderly, their bodies facing this way and that. With or without hangovers, their youth filled the room with energy and possibility. Most were graduate teachers taking a break before starting their careers in the UK. Some, like Archie and Catriona, were Italian language teachers and in *Bellano* to polish their aural and oral skills. Others were experimenting with an overseas teaching career.

A buzz of conversation persisted. Ralph raised his head and cleared his throat. Most of the men came to order by focusing on him but the women were looking at a spot over his left ear and smiling.

"Can we get started, please?" Ralph said.

There was an edge to his voice that slapped the staff to silence. Ralph cursed himself. Even Louise had become tense. In her role as Director of Studies, she was sitting to his left, her hand poised over an A4 pad, her face punctuated by an interrogation mark.

A newspaper crumbled and crackled, and there was a yawn from the languid body draped over a classroom chair. Middle-aged disapproval was evident in the tilt of Roger Wilmot's mouth. Ralph could not say whether this was due to Roger's own edginess or a cryptic crossword clue.

"A pistol that kicks, Ralph?" Roger said. "Four letters."

"Excuse me?"

Roger lifted a pen from the breast pocket of his jacket.

"Colt," he said

"And I have a class at 11 o'clock," said a female voice.

Ralph nodded at the figure tucked away in the corner.

"No problem, Miss O'Henry," he said, his attention attracted by the foggy wisps hanging over the window ledges at the back of the room. Miss O'Henry nodded in response and her grey-streaked hair swept her shoulders and her mouth smiled open. Adjusting his vision, Ralph saw Louise reflected in the windowpanes. Her shoulders were back, her head was up and scanning the room.

"Agenda today," Louise said. "Staffing issues,

photocopying problems, cheap holiday flights back to England, standby teachers, and Cambridge exams."

"And AOB?"

Ralph snapped his head up and cursed himself, as he always did, for overlooking Mrs Norton. On the two afternoons she taught her course in British Crime Fiction, the tap, tappings of her walking stick in the corridor were an integral part of the school. On two other afternoons, she looked after the British library in *Bellano*. The library was a hangover from those times when *Bellano* was a place to recuperate or a place to winter-holiday for those who lived north of the Alps. When Bella Norton alighted in *Bellano* in 1946, she would have heard English voices all around her. In 1989, the town was no longer on the international travel industry's A-list of destinations. Bella was now cutting her hours and preparing for her retirement in Bournemouth. Her intention was to spend her twilight days writing the one novel she believed she was supposed to write – a British murder story to surpass anything ever written. Good would triumph over evil and she would end the book with the suggestion that despite the pleasures of Italy, the British way of life was the best on offer. She had been jotting down ideas for years and had notebooks full of sentences and paragraphs that she just needed to stitch together.

A scattering of voices suggested points to be discussed under AOB but these were silenced by the confidence of Paul Loban, alias *The Lizard Man*.

"Nicky's not made it back, then?"

"Not AOB," ventured a voice laced with Scottish lowland brogue.

"Then, let us reconstruct the question, shall we?"

A titter of derision rippled through the room but *The Lizard Man* was not to be deterred. He flicked his tongue between his lips several times. The wet slapping that accompanied this movement was a signal that he was about to make an incisive point.

"I venture that his whereabouts in the evenings are a cause for concern."

Paul Loban had arrived in Italy on the trail of a whim in the 1950s. The whim in question had not expected him to turn up and had been frightened off, but Paul was reluctant to return to post-war Britain and illegal homosexuality. He treated the Italians like colonial subjects but the students liked his authoritarian style and both they and Ralph respected his knowledge of English grammar. His predilection for hotel bars, cocktail lounges and other establishments or gatherings frequented by the rich and fashionable was legendary.

"He was by the station last night," said the voice with the lowland brogue. "Integrating with the locals, I guess."

The voice belonged to one of two youngsters sitting in kilts in the centre of the room. After a couple of years in *Bellano*, Archie had ordered the kilts from Glasgow and he and his girlfriend, Catriona, wore them when they needed to ground themselves. Kilts affirmed their roots and the Italians loved them.

"Poor Nick's gone native, dear," said Paul. "There really is no hope for him."

"Gone native or gone to the dogs?" Archie asked of the air around him.

These comments brought a shuffle of feet to the meeting. Eyes were raised to the ceiling, Roger Wilmot cracked open his newspaper and Miss O'Henry's flicked her wrist and glanced at her watch. Paul clasped his hands, laid them in his lap and studied them while he twiddled his thumbs.

Ralph shook his head, swore under his breath and clenched his jaw. Louise's hand fell on his forearm in time to prevent an irritable outburst. He breathed deeply, surveyed his disorderly teachers and asked them:

"What's all this about Nick?"

The ensuing silence released voices from the adjacent classroom. A teacher was using repetitive drills to practise a grammatical pattern.

"I must have had a problem," the class chanted.

"He," said the teacher.

"He must have had a problem."

"We."

"We must have had a problem."

Tucked away in her corner, Miss O'Henry opened her mouth wide and said:

"Paul is trying to tell you, Ralph, that Nick has personal problems that may have repercussions for all of us."

Roger looked up from his paper.

"Bond is said to be Asian," he said. "Four letters."

Ralph let his eyes flicker from side to side over the floor as though searching for something he had lost.

"Are we talking about the same man?" he asked.

"Unfortunately, yes we are," Paul said. "After work he goes on the hunt."

"On the hunt for what?" Ralph asked.

Paul swung his nose into the air.

"The delights our Italian friends have to offer."

"Which are?"

"Ask Archie," Paul said. "That's his sort of thing."

Archie shifted and his face reddened.

"Watch your mouth..."

"Order, please," said Ralph.

"Thai," said Roger Wilmott.

Louise's fingers gripped Ralph's arm. They were firm, uncompromising. Then, she was standing at his shoulder – poker-faced, balanced; her voice crisp and incisive.

"Would you please tell us, Archie, who Nick was

37

with?"

Archie shook his head.

"A local?" he said.

Louise watched him, her face expressionless.

"Did you not see who it was?"

Archie looked around him for support but most of his colleagues were sitting back with their arms folded.

"It was too foggy for me to see," said Archie, his anger running ahead of his discomfort. "I think he went away with someone in a car."

Louise contemplated Archie for some moments. She then asked, very slowly:

"You say it was too foggy to see? Isn't it possible that you could have been mistaken?"

There were shouts of "good question," from the other teachers.

"They must have had a problem," cried the class in the adjacent room.

"I don't think so," Archie said. "He's so big and, er, noticeable."

"You don't think so? Which features in particular do you think you noticed?"

Archie shrugged.

"His height? He is taller than most locals."

"But not all locals."

"No, but I recognised his clothes and his Viking looks."

"Viking looks?"

"Yes, you know."

"No, I don't know. Enlighten me."

"His scraggly beard? His fair hair?"

"And was he carrying an axe and a sword?"

Cheers and laughter erupted from the staff. Ralph slammed his hand down on the table.

"Can we have some order?"

The hand on his arm squeezed again.

"Just one more question, please. Have you seen Maria Teresa this morning, Archie?"

Archie rolled his eyes to the ceiling.

"Yes, I have. And?"

"And can you please describe what she is wearing today?"

Archie opened his mouth but said nothing. Louise went for the jugular.

"Isn't it true, Archie, that you might have made a mistake? Isn't it true that you might have seen someone else?"

Archie looked around for support, found none and slipped both hands beneath his buttocks.

"I saw him," he hissed, isolating each word. "I saw what I saw."

*The Lizard Man*, Paul Loban, jumped to his feet, raised his hand and jabbed a finger at Ralph and Louise.

"The question is," he said, "what are you going to do about this?"

"I'll have a word with Nick when he arrives," Ralph said. "Now can we...?"

Paul wagged his finger and shook his head.

"No, no and no," he said. "Might I suggest that the scandal, of which many of those present today were victims, makes "a word" hardly appropriate. Action needs to be taken and it needs to be taken now."

There were shouts and mumbles of "hear, hear" from the older members of staff.

"I believe the matter should be placed on the agenda with immediate effect, in the light of what once occurred."

A defiant Paul resumed his seat and folded his arms.

Ralph fumbled for words. His authority was being challenged; he needed to respond but his mind got no further than the wisps of fog spiralling and turning against the windows at the back of the room. A shuffling sound made him look up. Mrs Norton was standing and leaning heavily on her stick.

"Mr Chairman," she said, "is this subject on the agenda now or not? If the answer is "yes" then I move that the item be discussed immediately. If there is any truth in these allegations of misconduct on the part of Mr Radcliffe, they are a matter of grave concern to all of us."

She was still on her feet when there was a knock and the door crashed open. Maria Teresa hovered on the threshold, shaking her head as though regaining her senses. Ralph greeted her with an impatience that was reflected in the tone of his voice.

"Yes, Maria Teresa."

He mentally slapped himself. The school secretary practically ran the school single-handed. More than that, her contacts with local bureaucrats and businesses leaders had been invaluable in the first years of The Conrad School. By 1980, they were in a position to consider renting premises in the centre of town. It turned out that Maria Teresa's brother-in-law was a property dealer and, with his help, they were able to centralise and administer their growing empire. By the beginning of the 1981-1982 school year, they even started hiring people.

"It's the copier," Maria Teresa said. "It's broken again. I thought you'd want to know."

"Then can you ring the services – again, Maria Teresa, please?"

She wagged her head, and Ralph noticed that her solid legs were failing her. He saw it in the quiver of her skirt, and the eyes staring at him were as big as saucers and full of something frightening.

"Is there something else, Maria Teresa?"

She nodded.

"Mr Radcliffe."

"What about him?"

"He's been taken."

From the adjacent classroom, a flurry of squeaking chairs suggested that the students were settling down to a writing exercise.

"He's been taken to the *Questura*," Maria Teresa said, "the police station."

"We know what it is, Maria Teresa," Ralph said. "Did Francesca go to the police and complain?"

Maria Teresa blinked.

"Your Francesca?"

"Did she go to the police?" Ralph asked.

Maria Teresa wagged her head and tutted.

"It's not Francesca. It's Nick. He's been taken away, arrested and charged."

There was a collective intake of breath and a chorus of questions from the teachers. *The Lizard Man* rose to the occasion.

"Quiet," he roared.

He sat down again and someone shouted: "Charged with what?"

"With murder."

There was a cry of alarm from Mrs Norton. Paul Loban shot to his feet again. Miss O'Henry held her breath and Roger Wilmot's newspaper slid off his knees and crackled to the floor.

"Quiet please," said Ralph.

Louise's hand was on his shoulder and while the staff shouted "yes" and "quiet now," she mouthed a word and pulled a face that asked him, "what's going on?"

Ralph took a calming breath and said:

"What's happened, Maria Teresa?"

In this moment of crisis, Maria Teresa struggled to put her thoughts into English words.

"*Povero ragazzo*. My poor Nick." She was shouting now, her face flushed. "He's been accused of murdering

*Signor* Merighi."

She staggered backwards and covered her mouth with her hands.

"It must be the usual groundless rumours," Paul said.

"Quiet, please," Louise insisted. "Please go on Maria Teresa."

"I took the liberty of ringing the police," she said through her hands. "A man has been detained and they told me a substitute teacher for the day should be found. Mr Radcliffe will be delayed."

"And what else did they say?" Louise asked.

"If they don't charge him, he'll be out in a few hours. If they formally charge him you will be allowed to visit during visiting hours only. You will have to wait I am afraid."

There were shouts of disapproval followed by a plea for silence from Louise.

"When are visiting hours, Maria Teresa?"

Maria Teresa shook her head.

"Can you please find out?" Louise said. "Please make the necessary calls and please do it now."

The teachers fell silent and eyed Louise with a respect that leadership qualities deserved. Everyone knew that Maria Teresa needed a framework in which to operate. The prospect of something to do pacified the school secretary and she swung round and left the room with a sense of purpose in her step. Nor were there any dissenters when Louise proposed a postponement of the staff meeting. The teachers, fidgeting with impatience, headed for the door.

"We need to act," Louise said to Ralph. "I'll buy you lunch in *Sommariva*. We don't leave there until we have a plan. Our priority is to Nick. We need to see him."

Ralph waved the minutes in the air.

"Let me copy these," he said. "I'll see you in *Sommariva* very shortly."

The first thing Ralph noticed was the throng of teachers. They had raced out of the classroom but had got no further than the entrance hall and were whispering amongst themselves. Her performance over, Maria Teresa was back at her desk. In her rightful place at the heart of the school, she had regained her composure in routine and was sitting with the phone at her ear. She caught Ralph's eye and signalled to him that he should wait.

"So," she said, replacing the receiver. "The Police will hold Nick for ninety-six hours. Visiting times are between 4 and 5 o'clock in the afternoon."

"Thank you, Maria Teresa."

"Nick has not yet been charged," she said, "but an extension to custody has been granted while investigations continue."

Ralph glanced at his watch and, grabbing for his coat and scarf, he made his way out of the door and into the stairwell. Buttoning up his coat, he rushed down the stairs, through the door and emerged in the fog. A group of onlookers, wrapped in their *loden* coats and scarves, had already gathered outside the school. He turned to see what it was that interested them.

Across the door and straddling the fine-brushed metal plate was written: "English murderers out!"

Rumour had condemned them.

# 5

Ralph tightened his scarf, pulled at the collar of his coat, and strode down the street with his shoulders humped to the slanderous accusations painted on the door. It was not the first time that being English had attracted hostility. During the Falklands conflict, someone – no doubt a relative of an individual who had uprooted and gone to Argentina in the previous century – had daubed the school with obscenities.

Ralph muttered an obscenity of his own and, for a moment, his stride faltered and he stopped to peer back along the street. He was hoping to see a red glow following him through the fog, hoping to hear the click, click of heels on the pavement, but he saw nothing except the fog swirling around him.

"Damned photocopier," he said aloud and, glancing at his watch, he set off again, faster this time, like a man with a mission.

Only when Ralph reached the corner of *Via da Modena* and *Piazza Lorenzo* did he pause. The *piazza* enclosed the Romanesque church of *San Lorenzo*. The church received few visitors even though the painting above the altar was alleged to be by Titian. In contrast, Gloria and Gina's, the establishment on the corner opposite, was full from morning until night. He watched the shifting shapes and shadows of its customers through the fog, the glass door and the two large oval display windows which flanked it. The oval windows always brought to his mind enormous spectacles looking out on the passing world.

Ralph crossed the street and, pushing at the door, he entered the public area of the place. It was dominated by a large table with heaps of paper and ink cartridges, home-made *grappa*, a coffee machine, drinking glasses and piles of folded washing. Under a staircase to Ralph's left was a large room with a table, chairs and a photocopier, which cast a regular light on the faces of the room's occupants. In a corner opposite the photocopying room was another table. It was covered in a sheet and carried an iron. Above the table was a payphone. To the left of the phone, deep in the interior, the place was full of pillars and partitions. The partitions divided the area into cubicles, each with its own table, old and darkened by shadows, whispers and secrets.

Clad in shawls and skirts, and with their white hair pulled back into buns, Gloria and Gina were sitting as if joined at the shoulder and hip behind the entrance table. Statue-still, with hands on knees, their presence dominated the activity that surrounded them. Although the two ladies lent their name to this establishment, nobody had ever attached a conventional label to it. Nor could anybody ascertain how long it had been there. It was part of the natural order of things along with Gloria's shaking hands and Gina's blindness. Everybody knew that the two women were at the heart of vast networks of communication channels. Gloria's and Gina's establishment was a kind of oracle – the place to go if you needed information or advice.

Rumour had it that the war and its aftermath had been good to them. Both women managed very good English – a present from American GIs in 1944. They were adept at adding an "eh" sound to the end of most words and they were unwilling to perform the necessary verbal acrobatics to change things. Ralph had heard suggestions that they had made a fortune after the war by satisfying the demand for counterfeit documents. It was said that Gina had paid the price of this lucrative trade by losing her sight. Nobody had ever dared to ask them about these allegations but the contents of the place suggested a background in copying and reproduction.

Whatever their trade, past or present, everyone admitted that the two ladies made a great team. Gloria used her eyes to guide Gina's steady hands to the bottles, the glasses and the cups. Gina's hands separated out the washing and ironed the shirts and trousers and Gloria's eyes guided her efforts from the pressed pockets to the lining up of the inseams.

Ralph loosened his scarf and played with his coat buttons until the light in the photocopying room flickered to a stop. He was walking in as a middle-aged man in a sharp suit staggered out with an armful of paper. Ralph flattened his back against the wall, but the middle-aged man walked past as though unaware of Ralph's presence. Ralph muttered an obscenity and scowled at him and the man smiled back revealing small but very white teeth.

Ralph was still fretting while the machine ejected his copies. He found distraction from his mood by focusing on the activity in the public area. New arrivals were easy to spot. They stood between the door and the heaps of paper rubbing their hands and unbuttoning their coats. Those who had already established themselves were barely visible in the cubicles, leaning forward in their shirt sleeves and conversing in whispers. The middle-aged man in the sharp suit was standing at the pay phone and gesticulating while he barked down the transmitter. Ralph glared at him, pushed his way out of the copying room and stood at the large table fumbling in his pocket for money.

"I don't want to hurry you," Ralph said, "but I have an appointment."

Gina rested her hand on Gloria's and they turned their faces in Ralph's direction, shaking their heads in unison.

"An important lunch date?" Gina said.

"With Francesca or Louise?" Gloria asked.

"Francesca?" Gina said. "But she just lost her father."

"She's beautiful and rich," said Gloria.

"Cold as ice," they said in unison.

"Please," Ralph said, glancing at his watch, "It's not..."

Gloria and Gina stilled their heads as though they had received a parade-ground order.

"You are right, Raffa," they said in duet. "It's not possible."

Ralph stepped backwards but the ladies' eyes followed him like searchlights.

"Nick would not kill nobody, Raffa," Gina said.

"And you must ask yourself," Gloria added, keen to impress him with her command of English idiom, "why this situation was out of the hand."

Gina gave Ralph one of the smiles she reserved for her favourite clients. Unguarded, the smile gave him an insight into a previous life of sight, youth, beauty and joy.

"How you not know your friend's life is on a blink?" Gloria continued. "He needed you and you put him down."

Gina lifted her hand from Gloria's and brought it down with a slap on the table.

"Back off," she said to her sister. "Ralph is a good man. Let him go and enjoy his lady friend, whoever she is."

Gloria turned her head towards Ralph and said:

"But we'll be watching you," she said. "And you better watch yourself. In Italy, when the push comes to the shove, difference become a problem and you are not integrated as you think. And nobody cares for you."

Gina raised her head and slid her hand under her chin.

"In fact, nobody gives a..."

"Give a man the break," Gloria interrupted.

Ralph watched the two ladies struggle to get the last word and the conversation fizzled out. He, at least, considered himself well integrated even if nobody mistook him for an Italian. He ran a successful business, spoke the language fluently, bought his clothes here, had his haircut here and made his contribution to society. But despite all this, he often felt like a fish out of water. He once thought it was his light skin colour, his dark blond hair and blue eyes that betrayed him. He doubted it now. It was more likely to be the way he wore his clothes and the rhythm with which he moved that gave away his English origin.

"So long, Raff, and take it easy, baby," Gloria said to him on his way out. "There are people with axe to grind on the Brits."

Gloria's finger continued to wag at him until he was back out in the biting air. It was barely midday but the street lamps had been turned on, and their light filtered through the fog and landed on the pavement as yellow puddles. Pocketing the minutes, Ralph put his head down and set off towards *Sommariva*. He looked up when he passed the school, but slithers of fog had thickened over the doorway and the graffiti was invisible.

He agreed with Gloria that anti-English sentiment was never far away. Some years previously while eating with Louise in a favourite restaurant, a man had walked in and, without introducing himself, had lectured them loftily on why Winston Churchill was an arsehole. Ralph knew immediately what the problem was. The memorial in *Piazza Del Risorgimento* was a constant reminder. Until his arrival in *Bellano* in 1976, Ralph had known little about World War 2 from an Italian perspective. The history books he had read at school in the early sixties had told him nothing about the sinking of Italian and German hospital ships by British submarines or the 2000 people killed in the accidental bombing of *Bellano* in 1944. The story was that British intelligence had received information suggesting that units of the German army were retreating through *Belluno* in the Italian Alps. Someone had misread and the RAF had bombed *Bellano* instead. The *Bellanese* themselves seemed to bear the English no ill will for this terrible accident even though there had be no German soldiers within 200 kilometres of the town.

Making a mental note that he should ask Maria Teresa to deal with the graffiti on the door, Ralph turned his back on the school and lifted his scarf to his chin. It was an instinctive but useless reaction to the cold. Experience told him that nothing would prevent the dampness from getting into his skin. Even by *Bellano* standards this fog was intense. Visibility was down to no more than a couple of metres and the further he walked from the school, the stronger was the sensation that the street lamps were the only other presence in the veiled and out-of-focus world around him.

Retreating into the warmth of his inner world, Ralph thought that his Englishness had caused him few problems – despite Gina's warning of push coming to shove. Being a foreigner was another matter. He had seen several people go to pieces in *Bellano*. It usually followed the same pattern and stemmed from the same loss of moral integrity. Foreigners had responsibilities and privileges. No longer bound by the restraining principles of your own culture, you were not always expected to conform to the values of the host culture. These privileges were a sort of freedom to be what you wanted to be. But this freedom came with a responsibility to yourself. Immersed in a moral vacuum, amorality could become a serious problem. Perhaps this had happened to Nick. His hold on morality had become so weak that he had slipped.

Force of habit prompted Ralph to step across the road at a pedestrian crossing but he walked smartly and with his hands spread outwards in the manner of a penguin. There was no sound of car engines, no sound of tyres crackling or wipers swishing. Cars and people might have been swept out of *Bellano* by a kind of Pied Piper employed by the town council to clean up the streets. Hugging the walls, Ralph occasionally discerned dark smudges slipping by him. Disembodied heads or shoulders emerged from the fog and reminded him that he was not alone. Clanging cutlery and clinking glasses moved through the fog and announced that he should be sitting down to lunch with Louise. But noises were distorted and Ralph was unable to say where the sounds came from. Even the street lights seemed to have given up the struggle. They had appeared at regular intervals but they had slid away. Ralph moved closer to the wall at his shoulder.

Skirting Bar Vittoria, he saw that frozen moisture had settled as a fine powder of frost on the metal chairs and tables at the entrance. The working girls had taken shelter inside and were preening and strutting behind the bar's glass frontage. The neon light above the door was somehow disfigured and resembled a deformed halo hanging in the air.

Groping his way forward, Ralph made a spontaneous decision to take a side road as a short cut to the restaurant. The feel of the cobblestones reassured him that he knew this road, that he had taken this route many times. But where there should have been an inviting light there was fog. Where there should have been warm welcome from Louise and one of their cosy chats, there was bleak silence.

Sounds nearby made him stop in his tracks. He heard the soles of shoes splashing over the road surface. They were hurried, urgent, and they were getting nearer. Instinctively, Ralph sidestepped but something unfamiliar brushed his cheek. He wondered at first if it was some kind of bird lost or disoriented in the fog. He hardly had time to register the ridiculousness of the idea when he heard the explosion of air from his lungs. He was hurled face first against the wall. It was like an unexpected rugby tackle and he would have fallen had the wall not been there. Opening his eyes, he saw beads of water running down the wall in front of him. Some of it rolled on to his nose, some dripped onto his chin. Somebody pulled his scarf loose and rough hands grabbed at his shoulders and spun him round. There was another hand across his throat. It pinned him hard against the wall.

Ralph was registering the presence of several shapes in scarves and hats when he heard a shocking noise that sounded like an animal in pain. It was a violent, choking cry. He felt his veins bulging in his neck. For a brief moment he looked into his assailant's eyes. "No, no," Ralph wanted to say: "You are not supposed to kill me. This is just a warning. You have misunderstood. It is only a warning." But Ralph knew the choking cry was his. It was useless to struggle. This man knew exactly where to put pressure and when to take the pressure off.

Ralph fumbled at his neck, trying desperately to remove the hands that were throttling him. The beads of water had run onto his temples and face. He wanted to shout out and tell them that they were not supposed to kill him. He was not supposed to die. The interview in London flashed across his consciousness. He was about to breathe his last and this is what he remembered.

"You've been in Italy for fourteen years," the interviewer had said. "Sunshine, sports cars and beautiful girls. Why on earth do you want to come back to the UK?"

The man released him. Ralph fell to his hands and knees.

*Sunshine, sports cars and beautiful girls.*

Saliva stretched from his lips to the ground. There was a voice.

"Ralph - Francesca is not for you. Keep away, understood?"

Ralph looked up. The Italian was heavily accented and suggested that the speaker was from the south of the country. He was looking down at Ralph. His face was hidden behind the scarves. His accomplices were behind him – shadows in the fog.

*Sunshine, sports cars and beautiful girls.*

"Hey, Ralph - understood?"

Ralph watched the man step backwards as if he were about to take a penalty kick.

"Yes, yes," he breathed. "Got it."

He watched the feet. They swivelled and tensed and sprinted away into the fog. Ralph knew they would not be back.

# 6

Ralph stayed on his hands and knees and concentrated on the place in the fog where the feet had vanished. He listened for sounds of movement but heard only his breathing and his attacker's warning going around in his head.

*Keep away from Francesca.*

Ralph sat back on his haunches, rolled his head and probed his neck with his fingers. He found no swellings and his breathing was normalising. But his heart was still thumping against his sternum and each thump came with a flash of anger. Smacking his fist into the palm of his hand, he winced and frowned at his knuckle as if it had rounded over some rare species of insect. He had been trying to ignore the blue swelling but the bruise was now thumping to the rhythm of his heart and blood from a cut was mixing with moisture in the air and running down his fingers.

*Keep away from Francesca.*

"Just friends... And what happens?" Ralph muttered.

He looked down at his fist and cradled it in his other hand while his thumb ran over his swollen knuckles.

"Jesus."

Listening for sounds of running feet, Ralph shook his head in movements that grew in confidence until his head was swinging in wide arcs.

"No, that's it," Ralph said as if to someone standing nearby. But there was nobody and nothing else in sight save the whitewash of brick walls and cobblestones around him.

Ralph pushed himself from the ground and swiped at his fringe. Straightening his coat and scarf, he rubbed his hands together and breathed deeply. Ralph had always thought that "phew" was a comic-strip expression, but he inserted his bottom lip between his upper and lower front teeth and the sound emerged as though from a catapult. Keeping close to the wall, Ralph set off towards a distant clinking of crockery and cutlery.

He was on the corner of the street, and alert and tense. A tap-tap-tapping of feet was approaching him in the fog.

"Please... Not again."

He ducked and raised his arms to protect himself but a black scarf and coat appeared out of nowhere. The scarf was wound around the person's mouth and nose, and the big brown eyes balanced on it were wide open. Ralph reeled backwards and he and the other individual glared at each other. Ralph was muttering a string of English curses when an arm emerged from the black coat and grabbed at his swollen hand. A muffled voice said:

"Stop it."

Ralph snatched his hand away but the person remained still, the eyes dark and calm. Ralph's irritation was turning into guilt that perhaps he was responsible for this near miss when the individual unwound the scarf. Francesca's voice said:

"Oh, Ralph. Still driving on the wrong side of the road?"

Without waiting for an answer, she stepped forward and rested her head on his chest. Ralph was paralysed. The sudden and shocking intimacy of her cheek on his body demanded an immediate response but his aching neck prompted him to look around and tune his ears to running feet. For a moment he stayed like a lamp post with his arms hanging at his sides. Slowly, he raised his left arm and let it rest on her shoulder. It was the sort of gesture anyone would make - a gesture of comfort for a young woman who had just lost her father; but Ralph was careful to let his right arm swing at his side.

"Your father," Ralph said. "I am so sorry."

"Shut up," she said. "Just hold me – with both arms."

Ralph raised his free arm. Her situation somehow trivialised his misgivings and he let his right-hand rest on her shoulder.

"Hold me," she said. "Keep quiet. I don't want to talk. There is much to say. I will deal with it in my time."

Francesca turned her head, leaned her other cheek on his chest and raised her left arm to let her hand rest star-like on his shoulder. Although aware of Francesca's bosom pressing against his chest and the smell of perfume on the clouds of her breath, Ralph was clear about his feelings for Francesca. Louise had once grilled Ralph about her.

"She's stunning," Ralph had said, "but objectively so."

He considered Francesca the classic Italian beauty – olive-skinned with a large Roman nose and long black hair, the fringe cut high above the big brown eyes. Below the neck, the classic Italian looks were less evident. The body was long and slender and she knew how to show it off with ankle-length winter coats and knee-length boots.

"What do you mean by 'objective'?" Louise had

asked.

"I am detached," Ralph had replied. "Looking at Francesca is like looking at, and admiring, a Donatello statue."

After his beating, Ralph now thought she was dangerous and contaminated. He dropped his left arm and tried to step away but Francesca was not going to let him go. She shifted her head and rested her forehead on his sternum.

"You must be upset too," she said.

"It's awful."

She squeezed his shoulder, sniffed out an inaudible comment and added:

"I can tell you're upset. Your heart is beating fast."

She raised her head, her eyes still closed. Her parted lips invited him to kiss them, almost overrode his desire for self-preservation.

"I've just been mugged," he said.

She drew her face back and snapped her hand to her mouth. Her face was deathly pale.

"Who by?"

Ralph raised his eyebrows and tutted.

"Who were they?"

"I don't know."

"You didn't recognise them?"

Ralph shook his head, lightly frisked himself and considered the lie he was about to tell. It was the second one that day. He had always lived by his father's dictum that lies were either a sign of weakness or an indication that something was very wrong. His father was right.

"They took my wallet," he said.

"Ralph, we must go to the police."

Ralph put out his hands, palms outwards.

"No," he said. "Fog is like darkness. Things happen that don't happen in daylight."

Ralph lifted a finger to the level of her mouth. It was

a gesture intended to ease her doubts and erase objections before she verbalised them.

"Let me take you home," he said.

She put her hand over her chest, her fingers playing with the buttons of her coat.

"I'm staying at *La Casa Rossa*," she said. Then she added, "The Red House... The one you can see on the hill from *Piazza Del Risorgimento*?"

In his mind's eye, Ralph saw the red house standing guard on the tip of *Monte Croce*. The slope of this hill seemed smooth from the town but in reality, it consisted of tiers that led upwards, one upon the other, until they reached the top. The earth was of red clay and the colour was reflected in pools of red light on the walls and shutters of the house. Under the shutters two arches gave on to a veranda from which a stone staircase, long since abandoned, dropped down towards the town.

Francesca turned her face away from his. A strand of hair clung with the fog to her forehead. Ralph noticed lines forming around the corners of her eyes. Perhaps she had not slept that night. He imagined her tossing and turning in her bed, her arms and legs thrown in all directions.

"It's the family summer house," she said.

She looked to one side of Ralph and her eyes flickered as if she were searching for movement in the fog. Rather breathless, she added:

"Buy me a drink in *Sommariva*."

Ralph looked at his feet and shook his head several times.

"No, I'm already meeting someone," he said. "I'm so sorry."

He hardly recognised his voice. It was so polite, he could have been talking to a stranger. Francesca tightened her lips, and her arms and shoulders lifted. She seemed on the point of screaming but stood blinking at

57

him until she pinched the fingers of one hand against its thumb, raised it to her chin and shook it. This was a common sight in Italy but the ferocity of Francesca's gesture was somehow beyond the limits of normality.

"Don't you want to hear about Nick?" Francesca said.

Ralph made a sound of hesitation.

"Then afterwards, perhaps we could go to *La Casa Rossa* for coffee?"

Ralph experienced a rush of excitement as another vision of Francesca in bed returned.

"The Communist Bar would be better," he said.

"Pasquale's?"

Ralph nodded. Otherwise known as the Communist Bar, Pasquale's had been a popular meeting place for students since the mid-seventies. At that time, the popularity of Eurocommunism attracted a lot of academic and political interest both in Italy and abroad. It was a flirtation with left-leaning politics that had also attracted Ralph to *Bellano* in 1975. Fourteen years later, his kindred Italian spirits had all but disappeared and Ralph had moved on to private enterprise and The Conrad School. He no longer considered himself a communist, but Pasquale had never quite given up his hopes and dreams.

Francesca hooked her arm in his and leaned into him. They walked briskly, and the sound of their coats rubbing together with a suggestion of familiarity excited him. It crossed his mind that the warning to stay away from her was also a catalyst that made her desirable and touchable. He lost the thought in the memory of her odd behaviour, her mood swings.

They mounted the steps to the entrance of Pasquale's, pushed open a glass door and went in. The bar was a single large room with communal tables all around it. Most of the tables were occupied and the din of conversation mixed with the sound of clanging cutlery to form one sound. Occasionally, the smoke in the air vibrated to the chants from a wall of blue and yellow scarves and flags gathered around several tables at the back of the room. Francesca held tightly to his arm as he made towards two empty chairs. Her warm breath was on his ear.

"I feel at home here with you," she said. "Don't you feel it, too?"

Ralph cheeks twitched. He was glad the walls were covered with framed photographs of football heroes past and present. He could turn his head away from hers, balance himself and smile.

Ralph was removing his jacket when a young waiter with permed hair pounced on them. He ignored Ralph and stood at Francesca's back while she unbuttoned her coat and threw back her shoulders to let the coat slide into his waiting arms. He hung the coat over the chair back and circled her like a matador looking for an opening. Francesca ordered drinks, dismissed him with a toss of her head and clasped her hands together.

"I was on my way back from the hospital," she said to her knuckles. "How would you feel if you saw your father's face smashed in?"

Her features were composed but the emphasis on the word "you" confused him. He touched at his fringe and straight into her eyes, he said:

"They say he was hit with an iron bar."

She leaned forward, lifted her arm and shifted his scarf. Her fingertips brushed his skin.

"You neck is bruised."

There was another burst of chanting from the sea of blue and yellow at the back of the room. They ended with:

"*Juve, Juve*, fuck off."

"It must have been terrible," Ralph insisted. "And

with such a weapon..."

Francesca shrugged, but her eyes were filling with tears and she placed the palms of her hands together as if in prayer and shook them back and forth in a movement that said, "What would you expect?"

Ralph responded by looking down at the table top, screwing up his eyes and biting at his bottom lip. Another roar from the blue and yellow wall at the back of the room drowned the "phew" sound that came from his mouth.

"Come on, *Bellano* – yellow blue, yellow blue."

"My brother is a fan," she said, scanning the faces of the supporters. "The *curva sud* is a home for him."

Ralph nodded but each individual in that yellow and blue group was faceless and anonymous. He looked up and smiled at her.

"Do you see him?"

She lowered her head and spoke to the table top.

"You probably think I am cold, don't you? You think I should be in mourning and wearing black, right?"

She hunched her shoulders, her big eyes getting bigger and sweeping the table top.

"Nick was covered in blood... found wandering around our house... How well do you know him?" she said, suddenly calm.

"How well did you know anyone? When you decide you like someone, you don't ask if they are capable of murder."

The young waiter danced back to their table. He slid two glasses in front of them, pulled the bottle into his groin and pulled out its cork.

"*Prego, Signora,*" he said.

Francesca waved him away.

"Father's death was a release," she said.

Ralph leaned forward and rested his forearms on the table.

"From?"

"From years of abuse. From violent mood swings. He was a tyrant. He ran the family and the company with a fist of iron."

She brought her hand down hard on the table top. The glasses sang and Ralph froze as the tremors ran into his arms and shoulders.

"Piero took the brunt of it. From the day he was old enough to talk, dad told him to shut up, that he was useless, would never amount to anything."

Ralph looked at her askance, decided not to unbalance her, to keep his questions simple. He was relieved he had not tried to kiss her.

"He's older than you?"

"Three years older. When mum died..."

"When did she die?"

"July 20th 1970. I was ten. When mum was alive, she protected Piero. After her death, I took over that role. When he was a teenager, Piero would disappear for days at a time – just to escape from his father's fists."

"Where did he go?"

"Into the mountains north of here. A place called *Monte Tomba*. He found a cave that had been used in the war by the partisans. Piero said it was like going home."

"Home was a cave?"

"The cave represented peace and security. He felt normal there. Now he gives his love to his dogs and to *Bellano* football club."

"Oh, what pure joy, to wipe your arse with a black and red scarf," chanted the fans.

Ralph blinked. The sheer bad taste of the songs never ceased to surprise him. Many of these supporters were quiet bank clerks or caring hospital workers but for a short time every week they dropped these individual identities and took on the identity of a group, in which normal manners and good taste had a hard time surviving.

"Do the police know that Nick was hanging around your house?"

"I had to tell them everything," she whispered.

Ralph nodded.

"And have you told me everything about your relationship with him?"

"We had drinks several times but he started getting serious and I refused to see him."

"And he started following you?"

"No, but he was always there. How did he know my movements? I dared not tell father about it. He hated the English."

"What did the English ever do to him?"

Gazing into her big brown eyes, Ralph turned his head as if he had been slapped, confused as to whether or not he had seen something not quite sane staring back at him.

"The bombing?" he said.

Francesca said nothing but she remained with her mouth open, her eyes darting from side to side, her tongue hovering. Eventually, she said:

"He was eighteen years old at the time. It was only in later life that he talked about it and only then because he was having vivid flashbacks."

She leaned forward, opened her arms, her head and shoulders twitching as though she was expecting a swinging fist.

"But if we had known how to read the signs, we would've known earlier. He was famous in *Bellano* for his fashionable appearance. He rarely wore items of clothing twice. How could we have known what this signalled?"

"I'm lost," Ralph said. "Start from the beginning."

"Dad and his parents arrived in *Bellano* with hundreds of other refugees looking for shelter and safety.

They heard *Bellano* was a safe place to go. Nobody could have known that a chance misreading of the town's name would end in slaughter."

There was a shout from the back of the room. The fans were getting restless.

"Turin, city of shit, to hell with the *Lega Lombardo*, red and black bastards," cried the fans.

"It started with the lights," she said.

"Sorry?"

"The lights. It started with the lights. My father always began the story in the same way. 'It started with the lights,' he would say."

She lifted both arms and ran her hands up and down in front of her as though scratching at the air.

"The lights, the sparkling lights, the beautiful lights like Christmas trees and bonfires lighting up the night sky. Then came the roar of the planes. Two waves of English bombers. In twenty minutes of bombing, the city was an inferno. A second raid came three hours after the first. He said it was intended to catch the rescue workers and fire-fighters in the open."

She looked at Ralph with eyes unblinking and licked at her lips with her tongue before scanning the supporters and directing her words to the back of the room.

"When the explosions started, my father's parents found shelter in a basement for their two children. They put my father there first and then went back for his sister. They did not make it. What he saw in his mind ever after were living torches glued to molten asphalt."

"Just a shout, just a shout, Turin in flames, Turin in flames," sang the fans.

"So, he stared into his family's eyes. Their skin burned and they screamed until their heads popped open. It was the smell...always the smell...the smell of explosives, burning meat, burning hair and burning clothes. He never got away from it."

"Wipe your arse, wipe your arse," shouted the fans.

"Do you know," she said lightly, "dad spent his life trying to walk the smell away."

She shook her head and waved her arms as though she was brushing away an irritating insect.

"You see? The smell followed him, would find its way into his clothes. He threw them away – those elegant clothes. 'Such a fashionable man,' the people would say. 'Such a fashionable man,' they thought. They had no idea about those images, literally burned into his brain, no idea about the smell that followed him."

Ralph stared at her, thinking. Refusal to talk about the past was something he had encountered with his own father. His experiences in the war had shaped him in ways that Ralph could only guess at. The outward signs that something was amiss were the bouts of depression – endless hours, the shape in the dressing gown staring at the bedroom wall while his mother hovered.

"Do you think Nick killed your father?" Ralph asked.

Francesca hesitated

"I don't know what to think. It is the violence that I don't understand."

There was her hand again, resting on his forearm. Ralph had visions of Francesca: slipping out of her coat, tossing and turning in her bed. Then he imagined the not-quite-human look in her eye and he shuddered.

Louise was at the door and staring at them.

"What is it Ralph? You look as though you have seen a ghost."

He threw on his coat, took the wallet out of his pocket and placed some notes beside the untouched bottle and glasses.

"I have to get back," he said.

He did not stay long enough to see the look of concern on her face. He did not want to look into her eyes at all. He was floating through the room as though weightless. He understood the feelings of a man who had been told his medical test was clear. Back from the brink of something unimaginable, he pushed at the door and rushed out into the street.

# 7

At first, it nipped at his ear lobes and at the end of his nose. By the time the cold had penetrated his shoes to grip at his toes, Ralph decided Louise would not be coming back. He glared into the fog, saw nothing but a memory of her face looking back at him over a bottle of wine in some shaded bar. He listened for her footsteps but heard nothing but the drip-dripping of fog and the quiet of the city taking its early-afternoon nap. In the stillness, erotic visions of Francesca returned and he allowed his instincts to drift along with them until they found their natural resting place with the girls in the Bar Vittoria. Ralph sucked at his bottom lip and then set off towards it. *Just one last time*, he said to himself, *just to celebrate my innocence.* Ralph managed a wry smile. He knew better than anyone that every time was going to be the last.

The first visit, he recalled, was just after his arrival in *Bellano* in 1975. At that time, he told himself that he would stop this behaviour in the future but the right time had never come. While he was building up the school, the future was some faraway place. Every week was an adventure. There was always something new, a new company, a new course, and new people to teach. There was no time for reflection, no time for remorse. Still, he convinced himself that one day he would change. But fourteen years had passed and although his visits to the Bar Vittoria had become a habit to him, Ralph knew that what he really wanted was a proper relationship and one that would have made his mother proud.

Ralph made his way down the cobbled street in which he had been attacked. Somewhere a car radio was playing, and an Italian love song drifted through the fog towards him. His mother had died in 1975. Immediately after her death, he swore that he would never betray her memory by giving his love to another woman. He had also sworn that he would keep pain and anguish at arm's length by never allowing another woman to leave him again. For fourteen years Ralph had managed to convince himself that the man who visited the prostitutes to satisfy his sexual needs was another person, a person he would eventually leave behind. Every time he went, it all seemed so harmless and certainly not a betrayal of his mother's memory. His sexual encounters came with the present and, until recently, Ralph had believed that the future would take them away from him. Now was crunch time. His secret was out. Someone had seen him here - completely by chance - and had threatened to publicise the fact.

He stood watching the lights of Bar Vittoria when they appeared through the fog. He saw his favourite girl sitting astride a table at the entrance.

"*Ciao, bello*," she said. "Want a good time again?"

Ralph remained motionless, incapable of turning from the shadow of guilt. He saw this prostitute through a golden glow. She was the embodiment of his depravity, his conscience personified. He could hardly believe what he was doing. If he only reached out for it, he could hold real love in real loving arms but he was letting it pass away. He had just stood her up, had left her to lunch alone in *Sommariva*. To make matters worse, Louise had come looking for him, had seen him with Francesca and then he had lost her in the fog. Pulling at the collar of his coat, Ralph turned and hurried away.

*

Ralph hovered on the corner of *Via Tommaso da Modena* and *Via Vittorio Veneto* and swore lightly. Under cover of the fog, he had been hoping to slip into the school unnoticed but there was a crowd, a dark and shapeless mass, round the front door of the school. He thought it might be groups of students on their way to classes, but shook his head. Groups of students were vibrant and energetic. The mass of people at the door was inert and hunched.

He peered to left and right, listened for traffic sounds and shot across the road. The people at the school door appeared to shift in the fog but, as Ralph approached, they shuffled towards him. Clouds of steam hung over their heads and filled the air with a faint smell of tobacco and *grappa*. Then, Ralph saw the cameras and someone shouted:

"Here he is."

The mass of people flowed towards him and Ralph sidestepped towards the policemen standing at the front door. A voice cracked out:

"Have you got anything to say, Mr Connor?"

Ralph stood at the policeman's shoulder while the crowd surged towards him.

"What can you tell us about Mr Radcliffe, Mr Connor?"

Ralph searched the jostling heads and shoulders for the identity of the questioners, but many of the journalists had covered their mouths with scarves. Speakers were anonymous and the questions came so quickly that Ralph stammered like a fool. He was glad of the policeman's presence, but Ralph's silence produced a resentful reaction from the journalists below and their interrogation became sharper and aggressive.

"How well do you know Mr Radcliffe?"

Ralph snapped his head towards the questioner, winced and rubbed at his neck.

"Why do you think he murdered *Signor* Merighi?"

But Ralph was no longer listening. He had seen the sign hanging over the door. It rested at an angle and obscured the word "out" from the recently etched graffiti, "English murderers out." The sign had a message of its own that made Ralph's stomach tighten.

"School closed until further notice."

The policeman was a young man, stern of face and thin-lipped. As Ralph disappeared through the door, the policeman took a step forward but a question followed Ralph up the stairs.

"Are you going back home to England after all this?"

The question was followed by a small cheer.

Ralph took the stairs one at a time, his mind racing. By the time he reached the landing, he had considered the implications of the assumption that *Bellano* was not home to him. *So, what am I doing here?* Ralph said to himself. *Having an extended holiday?* By the time he arrived at the entrance to the school, he was wondering whether home might be described as a state of the soul. Perhaps, he mused, where you were going was more important than where you were born. Home would always be the place you happened to find yourself.

Ralph pushed through the door into the entrance hall and babble of voices. He was adept at assessing the mood of a class by the hubbub that emerged from behind a closed door. There were babbles of expectancy and babbles of excitement. It was the word "apprehension" that sprang to his mind while he stood in the entrance hall. Maria Teresa was at the centre of a throng of teachers. With no students to teach and their role taken away from them, the teachers wandered around like sheep. Only Roger Wilmot, deep in a chair and his crossword puzzle, seemed unperturbed.

Mrs Norton was shaking her head and muttering something about "earlier-than-expected retirement." Paul Loban was trying to find an audience and pontificating on the Dunkirk spirit and the Indian mutiny.

"There are standards to which we must adhere," he was saying. "There are things to which we must never surrender."

His words floated off into the air.

"The police closed the school," Miss O'Henry said in a way that suggested Buckingham Palace had been blown up.

"Thank you, Miss O'Henry."

A voice emerged from the centre of the crowd.

"The police will see you tomorrow morning."

Ralph looked around and saw Maria Teresa sidling through the teachers. She sprang to a halt in front of him.

"Inspector Zantedeschi was here," she said in a tone that suggested Ralph should be impressed.

"Really? Is he a friend of yours?"

"Not exactly, but he is a fine young man."

Ralph smiled. He knew what Maria Teresa meant by fine. Young, good-looking and rich. No doubt he had charmed his way into the school and charmed Maria Teresa into giving him all the information he needed.

"What did he want?"

"He has already spoken to the staff but he wants to see you and Louise in your office tomorrow morning at

11 o'clock. He did say something about this being a 'self-solving' crime."

"Nonetheless, Maria Teresa, people are innocent until they are proved guilty."

Ralph looked up. Roger Wilmot had extracted a cigarette from a silver case and was in the process of lighting it. He looked through the smoke at Ralph and gave him a twisted smile before picking up the paper again and burying his head in the crossword.

"What did this man, Zantedeschi, want to know, Maria Teresa?"

"He is trying to build up a picture of Nick. He wanted to know if Nick had been having problems lately."

"I see."

"The school will remain closed until further notice," she said. "It is for the safety of all of us. *Signor* Merighi was well liked and well respected here."

"I saw the notice on the door, Maria Teresa."

"We must never surrender," said Paul Loban.

"Quite right," said Archie, who had replaced his kilt with trousers.

"The British government must send a gunboat to the Gulf of Venice," said Catriona.

"Inspector Zantedeschi confirmed what the *Questura* already told me," Maria Teresa said. "The Police will hold Nick for ninety-six hours. Visiting times are between 4 and 5 o'clock in the afternoon. So far, no charges have been made."

"Is there any other news, Maria Teresa?"

She looked down at her feet in the manner of a person who knows the worst.

"Rumour has it that the evidence against him is strong."

"Playing to the masses," said Paul. "They are nothing but a lynch mob."

"That sort of language will not help," said a voice

from behind them.

It was Stefano, the genial journalist. Ralph scowled at him. He was standing just inside Ralph's office and had not removed his coat. Stefano said:

"Come in, Ralph."

Ralph turned to the teachers and said:

"Unless you want to stay, you might as well go on home."

"Will you need me tomorrow," Maria Teresa said.

"Yes, please," Ralph replied.

"And don't forget," she added. "You and Louise. In your office tomorrow at 11 o'clock sharp."

Ralph shuddered.

"I won't forget. I promise."

Ralph brushed past Stefano and strode into his office.

"We needed somewhere to talk," Stefano said, "somewhere a bit more private. Can I ask you some questions?"

Stefano closed the door and hovered in the middle of the room at a midpoint between the desk and the entrance before taking a seat on the visitors' chair. He indicated Ralph's place and said with a smile:

"Sit down, Ralph."

Ralph unbuttoned his coat and, rubbing his neck, left the scarf on.

"You've got five minutes," Ralph said, sitting down at his desk.

Stefano leaned forward and folded his hands on the desktop. His eyes had a clear glint.

"You are still new here," he said. "You still have a lot to learn about Italians."

"I'm confident you're right."

"With your English eyes you probably see us as insincere – chameleon and prepared to change sides at the flick of a finger."

Ralph pouted his lips, separated his hands and

shrugged.

"You think so?"

"No? Well, you are different, no doubt. But the truth of the matter is that the people in this town will simply not believe that the murder of such an important person was anything other than the work of outsiders."

Ralph rubbed at his forehead with his fingertips before flicking several times at his fringe.

"I understand that the police had good reasons for arresting Nick. What did his foreignness have to do with it?"

Stefano unfolded his hands and, leaning forward, he picked up a book lying on Ralph's desk.

"*Great Expectations*," Stefano said, flicking through the pages of the novel. "People here might expect you to be reading Italian classics. After all, we are living in Italy. You should be immersing yourselves in our culture."

"This is an English school," Ralph said. "People come here to learn our language. Some are also interested in our culture. They do not expect us to teach them about *Dante* or *Alessandro Manzoni*."

Stefano slid the book back on the table, looked Ralph in the eye and smiled.

"Quite so," he said. "But don't you ever feel nostalgia for England, Ralph?"

Ralph pursed his lips and pretended to reflect. He and Louise often discussed England and what they missed about it. Both found that nostalgia connected them and was an effective antidote to loneliness and alienation. Ralph also found that those who had never lived abroad could not understand this. Stefano, he knew, had never left *Bellano*.

"No," he lied. "Italy is my home now."

"Well, I am glad to hear it," Stefano said waving a finger between his eyebrows. "But perhaps the people here will see this murder as an opportunity to take out their frustrations and prejudices. You know, the Italians are very tolerant of difference just so long as it stays far away."

"Which means?"

It was Stefano's turn to shrug.

"They look around and they see the beauty of their country and they ask questions like: what have the English ever done for the world? They have bad food. They drink too much and there is fog, always fog. No wonder they are cold and capable of anything."

Ralph remained unconcerned.

"Collective prejudice is hard to shift," he said. "Just for the record, I have never seen fog like the fog you have here in *Bellano*."

"But without the hound of the Baskerville's prowling around in it."

"Or Jack the Ripper." Ralph retorted. "Nonetheless, Nick is condemned as the stereotype Englishman, right?"

"What they see is a man who lacks restraint. Gone to the dogs you say in English. People say he drinks too much, that he has taken to drugs. Who knows what he might do while under the influence, don't you agree?"

Ralph leaned sideways and, opening a drawer, he took out a sheaf of papers, laid them on the desk and flicked through them.

"Sorry," he said, "what exactly do you need to know?"

"What happened to your hand?"

"Would you mind getting to the point?"

"You should have the hand looked at," said Stefano drawing out a notebook. "So, tell me Ralph, how long have you known Nick?"

Ralph reflected.

"Since we came here in the seventies. We set up this

74

school together."

"How well do you know him?" Stefano said. "What is he like as a person?"

"That's problematic," Ralph said. "If you ask ten people that question, you will get ten different answers."

"But you are English," Stefano said.

"So?"

"So, you must understand him better than we Italians."

"I don't follow."

"You speak the same language," Stefano said. "You share the same values, have the same background. You even listen to the same music."

"That may be true, but why make that assumption that I understand Nick better than Italians? Sometimes foreigners can see things in a person and in a country that locals cannot. We English can probably tell you something about *Bellano* that you simply don't see."

"An interesting point of view," Stefano said. "I'll keep it in mind. It might make an interesting article."

He snapped his notebook shut.

"We have evidence that Nick was often on the *equivoco* side of town."

"The shady side of town, you mean?"

"Exactly. Did you know this?"

"Nick never discussed it with me. He's adult, you know. Nick can choose to do what he sees fit as long as it does not break the law or have a negative impact on the school. This is our unspoken understanding. The school comes first."

"So, he never discussed these allegations with you?"

Ralph shook his head.

"Then, you need to reflect," Stefano said. "Perhaps you did not know him and cannot trust him as well as you thought."

Ralph looked back at him with an expression of

wonder.

"Interesting," he said.

"What is interesting?"

"Perhaps you'd better speak to someone who knows him better than I do. That might include any number of people out there who have already condemned him as a killer."

"Listen," said Stefano. "I have it in my power to destroy you. You are on your knees. You don't seem to understand what the press can do."

Ralph did not permit a ripple of irritation to appear on his face. Stefano was sweating. Beads of it were rolling down his forehead and his temples. Ralph pushed back his chair and crossed his legs. Casually picking up some papers on his desk and skimming through them, he said:

"Is there anything else I can help you with?"

A flicker of irritation appeared around the corners of Stefano's mouth. He took a handkerchief from his pocket and wiped at the sweat. He raised his eyebrows in advance of a question that was poised on his lips. Ralph interrupted by tossing the papers on his desk. He raised his hand and then leaned forward, both elbows on the desk, his head so low that he was looking up into Stefano's face.

"I would warn you not to write anything libellous in your paper. You should not forget that Nick has yet to be charged. Investigations are ongoing. Nick may have been having a hard time but he has friends – real friends and I am one of them. We English may be cold and capable of anything but I like to think we have integrity. If you start digging dirt on Nick, please think about Merighi himself. Do you think he was a saint?"

Ralph fell back in his chair and drummed his fingers on the armrests. Stefano said:

"What have you heard about Merighi?" He seemed genuinely puzzled. "It is my job to know everything.

Merighi was a hard-working and God-fearing man. If there was anything else, I would have heard about it."

Ralph smiled.

"We all have our secrets, you know? Why don't you ask the girls in Bar Vittoria? I've heard they might be able to tell you something."

"What do you mean by that?"

"It's probably just rumours," Ralph said. "Italians are very good at making them."

Stefano shook his head and smiled.

"If I heard anything it would be my job to investigate it."

"I am so glad you have at last mastered the conditional," Ralph said.

"It is like everything," Stefano said. "Application and perseverance are the keys to success."

"Perseverance, yes, I'm sure you're right. So - good day to you. And I hope to see you in class when the school reopens."

Stefano rose to his feet. His eyes flickered from side to side as he made his way to the door. He barely acknowledged Louise when she brushed past him and walked into the office. She was carrying a rucksack and a holdall.

Ralph braced himself for her view of his non-appearance at *Sommariva*. She would present this view in a way that suggested it was the only one to fit the facts and that any other was worthless tittle-tattle.

"I can't believe I wasted so much time," she said.

"I'm sorry."

"That damn woman; who does she think she is?"

"It's not her fault," Ralph said, "I am responsible."

"When I saw her after lunch, I thought I might hit her."

Ralph placed his hands on the desk and waited.

"Do you know what she said?" Louise asked.

"No, what did she say?"

"She said I was not good enough for her son. She said that we English should get out of *Bellano* before we could cause any more trouble. I can't believe what Tiziano did."

"What did he do?"

"He agreed."

"Agreed?"

"Do you know what? He has always loved his mother more than me."

"Incredible."

"What is it with you men and your mothers? Don't you ever grow up?"

"Just before it's too late, usually," said Ralph with a smile.

"Well, I have dumped him and left his house. Now he can stew with his mother."

"Good for you."

"The problem is," Louise said, "that I need somewhere to stay. I thought perhaps..."

"Of course, you can stay here," said Ralph, "but on one condition."

"Which is?"

"The police want to speak to us tomorrow at 11 o'clock. Will you be here?"

Louise nodded.

"I've been looking for you," Ralph said.

"Well, now you've found me."

Ralph glanced at his watch and got to his feet.

"Remember Nick?" he said. "Do you want to come with me?"

"To the prison?"

"It takes ten minutes to get there. Visiting times are between 4 and 5 o'clock."

# 8

The corridor had no windows and the smell of chemicals and sweat flowed down its length with the echo of their footsteps. The glossy walls and floor had a reducing effect on Ralph. He felt his individuality was being swallowed in a uniform of grey. Here and there, lights studded the ceiling, and Ralph imagined that they burned for twenty-four hours, indifferent to whether it was night or day.

The officer stamped to a halt. His left hand gripped one of a series of vertical metal bars while the other hand reached for a bunch of keys. They were hanging down from his belt and rested on the line that ran down his jacket to the purple stripe on his trousers. The key rattled in the lock, the door squealed open and shut behind them with an invasive clang that reminded both visitors and inmates they had left their privacy at the front door.

There were six cells, a set of three on both sides of the corridor. The cell doors, little more than large metal plates with peepholes, confronted one another in the manner of pawns on a chessboard. The officer stopped outside a cell to their left. He slid back the peephole cover, looked through it and grabbed for a key. He inserted it in the lock with a movement of arms and hips that suggested a grope of the crotch or a punch to the stomach.

The policeman stepped to one side of the door and, with a sweep of his arm, ushered Ralph and Louise into a stench of urine. Ralph was trying to look empathetic when the officer pulled at the door and smiling when it clanged shut behind him. Apart from a bed, a small table, and a bucket under the window, the only other notable object in the room was a light bulb dangling from a high, arched ceiling. A pair of plastic clogs was discarded by the bucket.

Nick was sitting on the bed, his unkempt reddish hair and beard contrasting with the pale wall on which his head rested. The prison trousers barely covered his knees and Ralph was struck by Nick's calves and ankles. He had never seen them before. The calves were graceful and hairless, the ankles thin and feminine.

"I expect it smells," Nick said. "I've been here a while. Missed the bus, did you?"

Ralph noted the emphasis on the flat vowel sound contained in the word "bus." Nick's use of strong Yorkshire vowels usually indicated that he was upset or had been speaking to his "folks" on the phone. In this world of prison trousers, prison shirts and prison clogs, the flat sounds were an expression of his identity. In the free world, Nick could use them as a signal of exclusivity, a rejection of people he did not always approve of – especially southern English, like Ralph.

"I wouldn't go into town for the *passeggiata* this afternoon," Nick said. "Not in these togs. Those oh-so-smart people in their fashionable clothes would stone me to death."

Ralph tried to imagine Nick taking part in the daily ritual he was referring to. As evening fell and the sun inched out of the *piazzas*, people filled the streets of every town and village in Italy. They were expecting displays of new romance and fashion. Nick's presence would have been a major disturbance, a slap in the face for those who took part in this afternoon parade.

"Wearing fashionable clothes?" Ralph said, recalling Francesca's story about her father. "You never know what their motives are."

Nick looked up.

"But nice to see you, Louise and Ralph. Now you too can have a few minutes break from your normal, busy, involved, and red-blooded lives, eh, Ralph?"

Ralph was struggling to put a smile on his face. He shuffled over to a barred window and looked out at the slice of freedom it offered. He blinked at the window ledge, the diseased pigeons pecking at the paint and bird droppings. He stepped sideways towards the cell door and, noting that the peephole was still open, he glanced through it. The narrow corridor and two of the cells opposite were clearly visible. He heard Louise ask:

"Have you seen a solicitor?"

There was an oppressive silence, but Ralph guessed Nick must have made a movement that signalled an affirmative because he heard Louise say:

"But you have not been charged."

Ralph turned away from the peephole in time to see Louise sliding onto the bed and Nick shaking a negative grunt from his mouth.

"I can't help them," he said, "I have no alibi because I remember nothing."

Nick looked into Louise's eyes and held her gaze for several seconds.

"I tell you, Lou, they could put me on the edge of the tallest building in *Bellano* and I still couldn't tell them anything."

Ralph knew what Nick was referring to – his fear of

heights. Once, when they had been friends, he and Nick had gone climbing in the mountains north of the town. Near the summit of *Monte Tomba*, Nick had frozen with fear. Clinging to the rock face and crying uncontrollably, Nick had prayed to a higher power to save him.

"What happened to your hand, Ralph?" Nick asked. "And your neck? You been fighting?"

Ralph lifted his arm and waved his hand in the air as if to dismiss both the question and Nick's concern.

"I'll tell you about it later."

"Yes, you do that, Ralph. I look forward to it. But I know what you are thinking."

"What am I thinking, Nick?"

"You think I was drunk, no?"

Ralph shook his head and turned sideways to glance through his peephole. The one in the door opposite was open. There was an eye behind it and it was looking right back at him. It flickered up and down and assumed an expression which seemed to ask, "Can we trust him, Ralph?"

There was creak of springs from the mattress and Nick appeared in Ralph's peripheral vision sitting on the edge of the bed.

"I was in the *piazza*," Nick said. "I start hallucinating. I go to the toilet. When I come back, weird things start."

Ralph tuned out. In those prison clothes, Ralph thought, and with that unruly hair, Nick could be any drunk picked up by the police and dumped in a prison cell for the night to sleep it off.

"A man materialises from a chair," Nick said, "and wants to be shown around the seedy part of town."

Ralph watched a finger appear next to the eye at the peephole. The finger tugged at the bottom eyelid in a gesture that chimed with his own suspicions that Nick had been drinking or taking drugs.

"I take him to the train station," Nick said. "The man

disappears and I start hearing voices from behind the bushes. There are creatures running about and people in swimming trunks."

There was a flutter of movement from the peephole opposite. The knowing wink that followed asked the question, "We're not so stupid as to believe that, are we?"

"Had you been taking drugs?" Ralph asked.

Nick looked up at him and scratched at his ankles.

"I don't do drugs, Ralph. Don't you know me?"

Ralph turned his eyes to the peephole. The other eye was still there and twinkling in amusement. Ralph swung round.

"How well do we know anyone, Nick? People change all the time."

Once the words were gone, Ralph turned his head away and looked across the corridor for a response to his non-committal comment. The eye looked up at him from a lowered head. Then it disappeared.

"So, let me tell you what you are thinking," Nick said.

"Please do," said Ralph, calling off his search for the missing eye and glancing at Nick.

"You think that I've changed. You think that since Annie left, I've lost it, right?"

Ralph shifted his head sideways. To his relief he saw the other eye slide back into position at the same time as his own.

"Yes," Nick said, "I can see that is exactly what you think."

Ralph opened his mouth but movements from the peephole silenced him before he uttered a sound. While Nick droned on about ripping leaves from bushes because they developed into human heads, the eye at the peephole turned in profile. The sideways slant of the eyes filled Ralph with feelings of uncertainty.

"I remember nothing about being in a car," Nick said, "but the next thing I recall, I am outside Merighi's house. I am vomiting and a policeman comes and takes me away. I am covered in the man's blood. They take my clothes."

He looked down at his trousers and twisted round to face Louise.

"They say I was wandering around his house, don't they? I don't know... I have just fragments of memory of places and people..."

"Which people?" Ralph asked.

Nick shook his head and, almost to himself, he said:

"Why would I be near that house?"

Ralph glanced at the peephole opposite. The eye, stern and unmoving, was now challenging him to act. Ralph pushed himself away from the door and stepped forward.

"Francesca came to see me yesterday evening."

Nick looked up. Ralph was standing square above him with his thumbs hooked into the belt of his trousers.

"She said you were stalking her."

Nick leaned forward and lowered his feet to the floor.

"That's not quite true," he said.

"Then someone's lying, Nick."

Louise stirred, glanced at Ralph in a way that told him to back off.

"I know what is going through your head, Ralph," Nick said.

"So you keep saying. So - tell me - what is going through my head?"

Louise rested her hand on Nick's forearm. It was a tender gesture but Nick threw it off, jumped up and faced Ralph nose to nose.

"You're thinking 'he's guilty,' aren't you? Well, well, Ralph how convenient for you. What is my sentence, arsehole? Banishment?"

Ralph flicked his head to one side in the manner of a boxer looking to his corner for advice. But his peephole was far away and Louise had shuffled upright, turned her head from one man to the other and put her hands between them.

"Stop this, now," she said. "I simply won't have it."

There was no immediate response. The eyes of both Nick and Ralph were locked together in a tight struggle. Eventually, Nick sat down on the edge of the bed but he kept his eyes fixed on Ralph.

"Hasn't he told you about our differences, Lou?" Nick asked.

Nick nodded into the ensuing silence. He turned his face to the narrow window and then looked down at his hands. He frowned and rubbed at his fingertips, moulding them, perhaps reshaping them. Almost to himself, he said:

"About three months ago, Francesca invites me for a drink after work. It's a friendly invitation and nothing more. After that, we often go out together. Nothing happens. It's harmless... just a bit of fun..."

Ralph glanced at Nick's hairless calves and said:

"Really?"

"My feelings for her change. I look forward to our little drinks, to seeing Francesca. I soon realise I'm falling in love with her. It's ridiculous. She's a student. This is not a relationship I want on the rebound. I decide to stop seeing her. It's too soon after my marriage breakup."

"And?"

Nick turned his head and looked directly at Louise.

"All the time, she's really interested in someone else."

"Who?" Ralph said.

Nick continued to stare into Louise's eyes as though he was holding a lifeline.

"She always talks about Ralph, Lou."

He looked up and allowed his eyes to re-engage with Ralph's.

"Yes, you, Ralph. She wants to know everything about you... The most pathetic thing is I'm encouraged to think she really likes me and, poor fool that I am, I believe everything I'm told."

Ralph glanced through the peephole and looked to the eye for help. There was just an empty hole.

"I don't follow..."

"Love and hate make people do peculiar things, Ralph. Perhaps she is in love with you."

Nick looked at Ralph with a long and unsmiling expression.

"Poor Nick. Poor Ralph. The tragic, wounded and manipulated heroes, who don't know what's happening to them."

There was a knock on the door and a face with a watch next to it. Louise slipped to her feet and promised to come again the following day.

"With grapes, perhaps."

"You are not allowed to bring anything, Lou," Nick said.

He looked at the floor and then nodded to himself.

"Right," he said. "You'll probably find Francesca at *La Casa Rossa*."

He turned his back on both of them and, stretching out on the bed, he stared at the ceiling. The door was already swinging when Nick shouted:

"Oh, Ralph, you didn't tell me about your hand."

But the door clanged shut and the officer led them towards the barred door. Ralph glanced at the door opposite Nick's cell.

"Who is in that cell?" Ralph asked.

The officer reached for his keys. He did not look at Ralph when he said:

"People are behind bars for many reasons," he said. "Most of them have broken the law. But we don't discuss them or their alleged crimes with anyone, understand?"

# 9

Ralph put the Alfa into third and his foot down on the accelerator. He raced through the narrow streets, his cheeks vibrating to the pounding of tyres on the cobblestones. Swishing back and forth, the wipers juddered across the windscreen and, together with the road noise, discouraged conversation. Ralph changed down to second when he felt the road steepen. He leaned forward, dipped his lights and followed the beam into the fog.

Soon, a canopy of stars appeared, and the fog thinned to wisps curling over the tarmac. Ralph switched off the wipers and the car lifted its nose and surged up the road that twisted to the top of *Monte Croce*. For a minute or so, he concentrated on attacking the straights and accelerating on the curves. Then, there was a voice from the bundle of overcoat and scarves in the passenger seat.

"I had no idea you could drive like this."

"Like what?"

"With passion," Louise said.

Ralph smiled.

"Dad taught me to drive," he said. "He loved speed.

He was a pilot in the war."

He changed down again, roared round a curve and into the next straight and the darkness of night. Glancing sideways, Ralph made out the stream. Catching the light from the moon, it was twinkling its way into the valley. When the engine noise decreased, Louise said:

"Both your parents are now dead, right?"

Ralph nodded.

"They died in a car accident. Dad was driving."

"When?"

Ralph raised his eyebrows.

"Just before I came out to Italy in '75."

Louise tried to catch his eye, but Ralph was staring through the window and remembering. For a long time after the accident he would see his father's face and one of his rare smiles, and he would hear his mother's laughter and her voice telling him that all would be well. He liked to think that, over the years, the loss had developed into memories that he could cherish for the rest of his life. They were constant companions and prompted random smiles throughout each and every day. He still found himself wanting to pick up the phone and tell his mother about his success in *Bellano*.

"Were you close to your parents?"

Ralph nodded.

"I was an only child. For as long as I can remember, there were just the three of us. When dad came home from the war, he had lost all belief in hierarchy – obeying orders and that sort of thing. He thought that the most important thing you could give your children was love."

Ralph changed down, accelerated round another hairpin and sped along the straight. He looked upwards. The shadow of *La Casa Rossa* was visible against the night sky and occasionally they passed the lintels, now disappearing in weeds and moss, that marked the remains of the staircase leading down from the house to the town.

"And did you get the love?"

"I was very close to my mum."

"And your dad?"

The springs in Ralph's seat popped as he shifted his weight. For a short while, he stared through the windscreen in silence. Eventually, he said:

"He loved me too, in his way. But as dad got older, he suffered from bouts of severe depression. He'd get flashbacks to his time in Italy in '43 and '44 – flashbacks about things he saw and did with other men - men he never saw again and things it might have been a blessing to forget. He was at *Monte Cassino*. He never talked about it."

"Do you know why not?"

Ralph shrugged.

"Perhaps he didn't want to upset us. Maybe he couldn't face the things he'd seen and done. As time went by, he often talked of ending it all. I have often wondered if he deliberately drove the car..."

Louise shifted and nudged Ralph hard with her elbow.

"Don't say it," she said.

"He might..."

"Shut it. Don't go there."

Ralph shook his head.

"It's too late," he said. "I've already been there, time and time again."

"The what-if scenario is of little help," Louise said.

"How can you avoid it?"

He watched her snap her head away and lean into the passenger door. She stayed there for some moments and then turned her face to his. Her cheeks were moist and her eyes were brimming with tears.

"You need some evidence," she said. "Without

evidence you know nothing."

Ralph turned and caught Louise's eye before she turned her head away.

"I understand," he said. "But sometimes, you just..."

"Just what?"

"You just know."

There was a brief silence, as if Louise did not want to respond. Then, her eyes brightened and she pointed through the windscreen.

"So, what's that?"

"What's what?"

"Over there," she said, pointing at some spot in the distance.

Ralph pulled into an area where the road curved sharply and widened enough for cars to park. He braked hard and the car shuddered to a halt throwing stones and grit flying in all directions. Nosing the car up to the crash barrier, Ralph switched off the engine. He and Louise got out of the car and stood fingering at the buttons of their coats while the engine cracked and crackled in the cold night air. Ralph turned his head in the manner of an animal that has caught wind of the hunter and then looked up to the sky. Stars and a piece of the moon appeared and disappeared through tears in the clouds. Below them, a number of hilltops rose through the fog and formed islands in the night. Each island seemed stabbed with fire. Louise plunged her hands deep into her coat pockets.

"What's the date today?" she asked.

"January 5."

"It's the night the witch *Befana* comes," Louise said.

"So goodbye to the old year and hello to the new."

They leaned towards the islands as if to hear the crackle of the flames and the yells of the children. In some cases, the village bonfires were so close together that they seemed to have grown into big ones that threw their sparks high into the air.

"*La Befana* brings sweets and things for the kiddies, doesn't she?" Ralph said.

"That's right."

"And they burn her for her pains? What sort of reward is that?"

"It's only symbolic, Ralph. And they say those sparks tell you your destiny."

"Then, mine will be bright," Ralph said.

"And mine is full of fire," she said. "I like it like that."

Ralph turned and tried to find Louise's eyes with his.

"Then, maybe, I can light..."

Ralph was interrupted by a series of flashes and bangs that filled the shadowed spaces between the fires. Rockets raced upwards, flashed, and then simmered as more fireworks followed their trails into the sky.

They remained in silence for a while until Ralph said:

"Do you hear that?"

He turned an ear in the direction of another sound. To him, it resembled the beating of a heart. Occasionally, he thought he heard the boom, crump, crump of drums. Ralph scanned the layer of white below them until he saw, directly over *Bellano*, that the heart of the fog was glowing. Every now and then, there was a boom and a flash of light. After the flash, the glow reddened and patches of dark and coloured cloud drifted into the night sky.

"It's the football stadium," Louise said. "The game is underway – fireworks and all."

Immediately over the stadium, the sky was now red and angry, and pinkish-white smoke ballooned in a great cloud. Louise leaned forward, shivered and then stood upright. Tossing her head, she allowed her hair to free itself from her shoulders and to fall down her back.

"What on earth was going on there in the prison?"

she said to the void in front of her. "What has happened to you both? And please don't tell me it's none of my business, Ralph. It is my business."

Ralph glanced at her. Her face was expressionless and her voice, flat and empty of emotion, told him that Louise had assumed her role as inquisitor. He said to the ground:

"Francesca came to see me last night, told me Nick was stalking her. Nick said he wasn't. So, what is going on?"

"Ralph, that's not quite true. Nick neither confirmed nor denied your accusations of stalking."

"Not my accusations."

"Sounded like it, Ralph. You were hard on him." She was fingering a coat button again, wrapping her finger around it and pulling. "It's bad enough that Nick has lost his freedom. He has also lost his autonomy, his friends, his privacy and his choices. Don't you think he needs some kindness? Why do you go around wearing a suit of armour all the time?"

The button broke away and, with an exclamation, Louise threw it to the ground. Ralph reacted with a show of detachment but his words of excuse sounded lame to him.

"I wanted to get at the truth," he said.

Louise moved towards him, her feet shuffling. The expression in her eyes seemed caught between the smile on her cheeks and the lines that creased her forehead.

"The truth is not always cold and logical," she said. "It contains feelings, too. Don't feelings matter, Ralph?"

Ralph looked at her. His face was as near to blank as he could make it when he took a deep breath and said:

"There are things happening between me and Nick. It started just before Christmas."

Encouraged by her silence, Ralph told her that serious competition to The Conrad School was emerging in the shape of a British Council annexe due to open in *Bellano* in April that year. She listened in silent concentration when he told her that he and Nick had disagreed strongly over their response to the threat. Nick wanted to differentiate The Conrad School by making it a centre for Discovery Learning.

"And I think we need to stay flexible. Nick is adamant. He says that if we can't agree he'll resign and set up a centre of his own and take his classes with him. That means all our company courses and their revenues will go with him."

"There are three owners here," Louise said, her face showing no emotion. "I am one of them. Did nobody think of discussing this with me?"

She looked out over the cloud, while Ralph mumbled an apology. Eventually, she said:

"Doesn't sound like Nick to be so inflexible. Is there nothing else eating away at you both? Jealousy, perhaps?"

She raised her eyebrows at his silence but her lips were narrow and barely moved when she said:

"Come on Ralph. Cat got your tongue?"

She silenced Ralph's objections by lifting her chin and tucking a strand of hair behind her ear.

"What did Nick mean?" Louise said. "He referred to 'Poor Nick. Poor Ralph. Tragic, wounded and manipulated.' Are you being manipulated, Ralph?"

Ralph rubbed at his neck and then at his knuckles.

"Why would anyone do that?" he said, spinning round and sliding back into his car. For several seconds, he watched Louise fingering the remaining buttons on her coat and looking towards the light over the stadium. Louise then raised her head to the sky, took a deep breath and turned towards the car.

"We can't run this school unless we are open and honest with one another," Louise said, slamming the door. "It simply can't be done. Am I being clear, Ralph?"

Ralph started the engine and backed out onto the tarmac. Louise placed her elbow on the arm rest, nestled her chin into the palm of her hand and looked obliquely through her window. They continued to drive for a few minutes in silence and without exchanging glances. When they reached top of the hill, the road widened again to form a large car parking area in front of the house. Ralph nosed the Alfa towards the gravel edging and, putting the car into neutral, drifted to a halt. Switching off the engine, he pulled at the door handle and his feet landed on the gravel with a loud crunch. Pushing himself upright, he stood at the car door, feeling deflated and looking at *La Casa Rossa*. He was expecting a female voice to challenge him at any moment.

# 10

Loitering at the car door, Ralph eyed *La Casa Rossa*, now dark against the darkness. His thoughts drifted first to Louise's comment about manipulation and then to Francesca and the beating he had received that morning. He touched at his throat until a light wind blew a feeling of snow down from the mountains and through his coat. Ralph thrust his hands into his pockets and leaned down to whisper into the car's interior.

"Italy and rumours go together like black and white," he said, shoving the driver's door closed with his thigh. "Nick and I manipulated? I can't imagine what anyone would want from us."

"Maybe 'anyone' doesn't want anything from you," Louise said, but Ralph was no longer there. He was edging towards the shadows of bay windows and ornamental woodwork. The drums were still sounding from the stadium but at this greater distance they barely shifted the silence which weighed down on *La Casa Rossa*. The clouds of vapour pouring from his mouth made Ralph feel vulnerable. In order to slow his breathing, he stood stock still and focused his eyes on the pyramidal roof. Shining in the intermittent moonlight, the roof seemed to hover unsupported in the night sky and, below it, perhaps in an attic room, a light was glowing.

Ralph was stepping up to the veranda when the Alfa's passenger door clicked open. He stopped dead in his tracks and half-turned towards footfalls on the gravel behind him. He remained still, waiting for Louise and taking in his surroundings. On the porch, a lantern hung down from between a double-arched ceiling and threw its light on the lower brickwork, a corner of the garden and its high, wire fence.

Ralph allowed his imagination to wander over the next few minutes with Francesca. He thought about the information he needed and how to frame his questions in order to get it. There was a rustle, a scrape of metal on concrete and two large shapes rushed at the fence from the garden shadows. He span round, found his own fear reflected in Louise's eyes, and then turned to approach the shapes hurling themselves against the fence.

"Whoa, boy," he said. "Whoa."

He accompanied these sounds with further words and comic movements of the arms that he had seen in the cinema. He found his efforts amusing but there was nothing funny about the animals' skin, glistening in the lamplight. Nor did the quiver of their legs or the bared teeth make him laugh. The dogs threw themselves at the fence several times until they retreated into the darkness and barked at the sound of the fence wire ringing through the air around them. The dogs fell silent when Francesca's voice called from the darkness.

"Who's there?"

Ralph looked upwards but saw nothing except some clouds running across the moon.

"Who's there, I say?"

Her voice now had an edge to it, an unspoken threat

of something unpleasant if he did not reply. In his mind's eye, Ralph saw the quivering legs and the gnashing teeth of the dogs and said:

"It's Ralph."

"And Louise."

"Wait," said Francesca.

Ralph heard a window thump shut in the darkness above him. With one eye on the garden, he waited for Francesca to appear. A key clicked in its lock and a door creaked open. Ralph was unable to determine the position of the door until Francesca's head appeared between the veranda door and its frame. Her face was pale and her black eyes seemed ringed by darker shadows. Francesca stared into the garden and said something that encouraged the dogs to drift away into the night. She did not move a muscle and remained in the light of the lamp as though listening to the beating drums. There was a voice at Ralph's shoulder.

"It's a difficult time," Louise said. "Should we come back another day?"

There was no immediate reply and no movement except the whooshing of rockets blazing their way into the sky and exploding. Eventually, Francesca said:

"Come in and close the door."

Reluctance, like an internal barrier, prevented Ralph from movement of any kind until Louise's presence stirred him and the two of them crossed the porch shoulder to shoulder. Ralph ushered Louise through the door and followed her into the vestibule. He pushed at the door in order to close it and ducked his head as if there were beams at head height. There were none. The ceiling was high and white, and arched over a room of shadows and corners and brown furniture. The white walls were speckled with brown plates and mirrors and brown tapestries depicting exotic places and creatures. The white-and-brown effect was broken only by the triangular tiles of white and red marble that covered the floor. A crooked table with four crooked legs wobbled in a far corner. Beside the table, a brown curtain was half drawn over a glass door. Rocking against the crooked table with its four crooked legs, Francesca was waiting.

Louise was browsing but paused in front of a large canvass on the wall by the glass door. The canvass depicted an important man in a swirling cloak. Louise looked up at his imposing presence and said:

"We are sorry about your father and hope we are not disturbing anything, but for Nick's sake, we need to..."

Francesca shook her head.

"I'm waiting for my brother to come back from the game. I'm looking after the dogs for him."

Her voice was distant and her eyes, flitting around, suggested she was not awake to her surroundings. Ralph now saw that the dark shadows around her eyes were actually the result of poorly applied mascara. It was a stark contrast to her face, all pink hues on a foundation of white.

"I like your outfit," Louise said.

Francesca steadied her eyes and fixed them on Louise as if daring her to say more. Louise remained silent and threw her head back to release her hair but, wrapped up in the coat and scarves, the hair was nowhere to be seen. Ralph wondered if Louise found the retro 1960s housewife outfit as odd as he did. It was true that the polka dot apron and matching head scarf might be connected to the witch, *La Befana*, and the makeup suggested she had been playing the clown and handing out sweets to the children in a neighbouring village. But there was something grotesque about her.

"Why don't you sit down?" she said.

To Ralph, this sounded like a rhetorical question. Louise was looking around the room for a seat but Francesca remained rocking against the table in the corner and made no effort to help her. Louise found Ralph's eyes with hers and raised her eyebrows. The eyebrows were like punctuation marks that followed the thought, "What the hell is going on here?"

Louise nodded at the wine and the plate of *Bellano* sweets on a table near the entrance.

"Am I right in thinking that you're expecting children to come and eat *La Befana's* gifts?" she asked.

Francesca said nothing. The metronomic click-clock of the crooked legs on the tiled floor increased in speed and, in a tone that was both a question and a reprimand, Francesca said:

"Ralph?"

Ralph smiled but Francesca became distracted and her gaze shifted around the room in the manner of a person who has woken up in an unfamiliar place. Ralph waited, his eyebrows raised. The room had already set in motion a series of childhood memories connected to his parents' Victorian house in Hampton Court. Sometimes, his mother would go shopping and leave him in the hallway next to his father's office. Left to himself, Ralph would play in a twilit area, full of mementos from the war and other paraphernalia. In retrospect, the hallway was always full of boredom and guilt. Ralph could do anything he wanted as long as he did not make any noise and disturb his father when he was having "one of his attacks." On at least one occasion, his father had silenced Ralph with a howl and a shout of his name.

"Ralph?"

"Yes, Francesca?"

There was a clatter of crooked legs on the tiled floor. Francesca slipped from the table and stepped towards him with arms akimbo.

"How is your neck, Ralph?"

Almost against his will, Ralph raised his hand and let his fingers run down his larynx.

"It's OK."

Francesca tossed back her head and looked down at him along her nose.

"So, who attacked you this afternoon, Ralph?"

Ralph shook his head. He tried to ignore the feeling that he was as responsible for Francesca's anger as he had been for his father's anguish. Francesca's searching gaze slipped over his shoulder and settled on Louise, before returning to Ralph.

"You haven't told her, have you, Ralph?"

"There is nothing to say. I was mugged and my wallet was taken."

"*Sciocchezza* - rubbish."

For a moment, Ralph was silenced by the snap of her voice. A gust of freezing air blew through the open door behind him and brought with it the scent of burning wood. It mixed with the smell of furniture wax to suggest the presence of mould or dark and damp locations.

"You had your wallet when you paid for our drinks," Francesca said.

She folded her arms and smiled her unspoken accusation into Ralph's face.

"Now just wait a minute," said Louise.

She turned her back on the important person with the cloak and stepped towards the centre of the room. Tossing her head, she looked at Francesca and then at Ralph in the manner of a duellist's second trying to reconcile the parties without violence.

"You were mugged? Can anyone please tell me what is going on?"

"Ask him," Francesca said.

Ralph raised his eyes, summarised his beating and downplayed its importance with shoulder hunches and shakes of the head. He finished with a stare into Francesca's eyes and said:

"I was warned to stay away from you."

Francesca's dark eyes suddenly seemed cold and threatening. She turned and weaved her way through the furniture towards a shuttered window. Raising a hand, she pulled at the blinds and looked through the narrow gap in the slats. Her continued silence encouraged Ralph to make a mild joke.

"Have you got a hidden admirer in the bushes?"

"Don't talk nonsense."

"Stay away from you?" Ralph said. "It doesn't make sense."

Francesca dropped her hand from the slats and remained with her back to him. She wrapped both arms around her and, in a tone that suggested both surprise and sadness, she said:

"Perhaps they mistook you for Nick."

Ralph shook his head.

"Who are 'they,' Francesca?"

Francesca unwrapped her arms, spun round and walked to the front door. With a powerful movement of the arm she slammed it shut and screamed out:

"I don't know."

Ralph was not surprised at the echoes set up by the slamming of the door. They seemed to have gathered in the attic rooms, sounded like light thunder and vibrated down through his body and into his feet. But he was shaken to the toes by the tone of her voice. For the first time in his life he understood the meaning of the word "wail." Slowly, patiently, he said:

"Somebody must've thought that I was bothering you in some way."

Louise turned her head towards Ralph and looked him right in the eye.

"Or that you were a rival," she said. "Did Nick see you as a rival, Ralph?"

Without waiting for a reply, she turned to Francesca

and said:

"Nick told us that you often talked about Ralph when you were together. Is this true, Francesca?"

Francesca bustled away from the entrance, her eyes sparkling with anger.

"You see?" Francesca said. "Nick was jealous of you. Perhaps it was he who warned you off. We know what he is capable of, don't we? You are lucky to be alive, Ralph."

Ralph shook his head.

"No," he said. "Nick would've warned me himself. No way would he have got someone else to do it."

"No?" Francesca said. "Have you considered his state of mind? How does a man feel when his wife and child leave him? Do you know? Did you ever ask him? Does he harbour a grudge against you?"

For some moments, the silence in the room was broken only by the sound of distant drums and rockets exploding in the sky. Francesca brushed past Louise and stopped in front of the important man with a cloak. She gazed at him for a while before lowering her head and studying the backs of her hands.

"Being with Nick was a pleasure for me," she said. "It brought me closer to you, Ralph, don't you see? I was able to sense you, your clothes, and your smell. You see, don't you? The fact that you shared the same nationality was enough."

"So, you did talk about Ralph," Louise said.

Francesca did not move and her pale pink face never changed its expression when she looked at Ralph but addressed Louise.

"I thought Ralph was interested in me. I thought he was holding back because he was afraid of getting hurt."

Ralph lifted his hand and stroked at his forehead before flicking back the strands of hair lying over it. Pushing out his lower lip, he said:

"Where did that come from, Francesca?"

Francesca turned her hands over as if she was a magician revealing an empty palm to a surprised and delighted audience.

"Piero told me," she said.

"What did he tell you, Francesca?"

"He told me you spoke to him about your feelings for me. It's true, isn't it, Ralph? Deny it if you can."

Ralph blinked at the light and airy tone of her voice but steeled himself for the fury he believed would come. Pushing his lip further out, he said:

"I have never spoken to Piero..."

He paused while receiving a revelation similar to that of Paul on his way to Damascus. No lights from heaven flashed around him and he did not fall to the ground but he heard his own voice finishing his sentence with:

"Never... about anything."

Francesca lifted her shoulders and curved towards him.

"That is your story," she hissed. "Your word against his."

Ralph looked down at his feet and held his tongue. He seemed to be deliberating with himself whether or not to continue. Eventually he said on a breath:

"Why would Piero tell you something that is not true?"

Francesca shook her head.

"Not true? Prove it's not true, why don't you?"

Francesca grabbed at her polka dot apron with both hands and pulled it downwards - once, twice, three times and each time a little harder until the tie at the waist snapped and it slid down her thighs.

"Why are you behaving like this, Ralph? Is it because of her? Haven't you told her about us?"

Despite the gusts of cold air, beads of sweat were forming under his hairline and the palms of his hands were clammy. He watched the apron drop past her knees and settle on the ankles.

"There is no 'us,' Francesca."

Francesca shook her head so strongly that the head scarf slipped down over her eyebrows. She leaned her back against the wall, pinched the bridge of her nose between thumb and forefinger and mumbled to herself with a dreamy smile.

"And daddy hated me for it."

"For what?"

"Spending time with the English."

"Because of what happened in the war?"

Francesca looked at the ground and shrugged.

"The war made him what he was and dictated the sort of father he became. In many ways, Piero is the result of events that happened before he was born."

"Believe me, Francesca, I've never spoken to Piero about you. It's simply..."

A slight movement suggested that Francesca was about to push her body away from the wall and attack him. But it was only her head twisting sideways and her eyebrows arching over the poorly-applied mascara. She said:

"So, he's a liar? How dare you? I've known him all my life. But you, you're insignificant."

This time Francesca did push her body away from the wall and she rushed toward Ralph with her arms flung in the air and her eyes shimmering with spite. She stopped just in front of him and looked him up and down from head to ankles.

"Why are you lying to me? To protect Nick? Nick? He killed my father."

"Actually, we have just paid Nick a visit," Louise said.

Francesca snapped her head in her direction.

"And? What did he have to say for himself?"

"He was surprised when Ralph told him about your accusations of stalking. He told us that he was encouraged."

Francesca's ears and scalp shifted but her lips hardly moved when she said:

"To stalk me? Are you mad?"

"He told us he wanted to stop seeing you but that you encouraged him."

"Confusing, isn't it?" Ralph said. "Nick said he wasn't stalking you and you say he was. Who is right?"

Francesca stared in front of her as if she had seen a ghost.

"You had better leave," she said.

There was something about her jaw that suggested the conversation was now over. An ill-defined feeling of unease spurred Ralph into activity. He grabbed at Louise's arm and ushered her out of the door while muttering their apologies for disturbing Francesca at such a difficult time.

Not a rattle of chains followed them across the veranda. Louise pulled at Ralph's arm and forced him to stop on the edge of the road near the car. The air was cold and Ralph knew there was a town below them, living and breathing beneath the fog. He needed to feel its familiarity, its normality. He leaned forward and imagined the sound of cars and normal people murmuring in the *piazzas*, cafes and bars of *Bellano*. Louise squeezed at his arm and whispered in his ear:

"Turn around, slowly. What do you see?"

Ralph turned and looked up the road and towards the house. Caught in the light, the still and sombre figure of a woman dressed in an apron and head scarf was visible on the edge of the porch where it met the garden fence. She raised her arms and shoulders in a questioning gesture and followed it with a shake of her head. Ralph shrugged.

"Can't say," he said. "It looks like Francesca talking to the dogs."

"You don't see someone else?"

Squinting into the darkness, Ralph saw the shapes of trees and bushes but he thought it was tiredness that made the trees and bushes appear to move.

"She'll be OK."

"That's not what I asked," Louise said.

"I don't see anyone else."

"No secret admirer hiding in the bushes? Someone she was expecting? Someone who wanted her to dress up in that ridiculous outfit? Her brother Piero, perhaps?"

# 11

"It's delightful to see you this morning, *Signora*, delightful. Please excuse my asking but, who exactly are you and what are you doing here?"

Ralph wondered where he had seen the inspector before. The man's English competence suggested that he had never before set foot in his office in The Conrad School; but wherever Ralph had seen him, the inspector had not been wearing his fashion statement - a pair of sunglasses – propped on his forehead like a headband. His designer jeans and unbuttoned white shirt could have been the clothes of everyman. In his early forties, everyman might have been on his way to impress the ladies in *Piazza Risorgimento* with a display of chest hair. The state of the current weather, Ralph knew, was of scant importance.

"I am Louise Middleton, part owner of this school."

The inspector lifted his shoulders, raised his chin, and emitted a sound like a truncated bleat. Whether the emotion it expressed was positive or negative was open to interpretation.

"And you live here with Mr Connor?"

"I've left my boyfriend," Louise said. "I'm staying with Ralph until I find another place to live."

Ralph had rarely seen Louise blush but Inspector Zantedeschi from the *Polizia di Stato* was not what they had been expecting. He had appeared shortly after 11.00 while Ralph and Louise were in the flat. Maria Teresa, who had arrived for work, despite the fact that the school was closed, knocked on the door to tell them.

"He was weak," Louise said. "He couldn't stand up to his mother."

The inspector rolled his eyes and bleated again.

"But when Nick was arrested yesterday," Louise continued, "it became intolerable. His family had been waiting for the opportunity to blame me. Just because Nick is English does not make me guilty by association."

The inspector strolled across the room and half-turned when he reached the window. In contrast to the fog at his back, his hair and eyes were jet black. The hair was short, oily and permed to the latest style.

"Please, do sit down," he said, pointing to the two chairs at Ralph's desk. "And count your blessings."

While Ralph and Louise sat down, the inspector swung away from the window and bustled around the room. Ralph was still trying to recall where he had seen Zantedeschi before. It was his air of subdued authority which touched some memory. He watched him stop at the bookcase and run his fingers down the spines of several books. He then slipped his hands into the pockets of his designer jeans and said:

"When Italy and Britain went to war in 1940, there were at least 19,000 Italians in Britain. Churchill ordered that they all be rounded up."

He smiled, showing small but very white teeth and the dim light of memory brightened. Of course, Ralph had seen this man in the photocopying room at Gloria and Gina's the previous day. He somehow hoped that the inspector had forgotten the incident.

"And this," Zantedeschi said, "was despite the fact that most of them, like my grandfather, had lived in Britain for decades. The police turned a blind eye as the mob looted and destroyed their homes and shops."

He was off again, pacing around the room. Ralph noticed that, despite his vigour, the inspector kept bodily movements to a minimum. His head and neck were still, his back straight but his eyes were everywhere.

"That's all history," said Louise.

The inspector whipped round to face them.

"No, it's a warning," he said. "Foreigners are accepted in most countries until something happens, for example: a war; an economic crisis or a murder. Then you find, all at once, you are not so popular and not as integrated as you think. Perhaps you would now agree, *Signora* Middleton?"

The striking of the hours from the church of *San Lorenzo* prompted Ralph to look through the window. The world outside was whitewashed from vision and a faint murmur was the only indication that there was any life in the streets.

"And *Signor* Merighi was a well-liked citizen," the inspector said. "He was a model to many people here."

As if to underline this statement, there was a shout of greeting from the street below. This was followed by another, the opening gambits of a conversation and gales of laughter.

"A model citizen?" Louise asked.

The inspector leaned over the table in a corner and leafed through some English magazines.

"When I was a little boy," he said to the table top, "one half of this city was still lying in rubble. This was the area between the station and the city wall. It was bombed in the war. *Signor* Merighi was a man from a humble background who profited from post-war reconstruction."

"Is this why the school has been closed?" Louise asked.

"A nice use of the passive voice," the inspector said. "Actually, I ordered the closure of the school."

He slid the magazine he had been holding back onto the table and adjusted the sunglasses on his head.

"As I said, *Signor* Merighi was well respected and well liked. When Mr Radcliffe was arrested, we had to think of public order. The safety of people in this town is my responsibility."

He lowered his arm and held it akimbo on his hip.

"What would you have done, *Signora*?"

"When can we reopen?" Louise asked.

The inspector raised his shoulders again.

"When the authorities deem it safe to do so."

"So," said Louise, "the school will remain closed until you say it can reopen, right?"

The inspector smiled but his black eyes were pinpricks of light.

"I have an investigation to complete. Evidence is being collected and suspects are being interviewed."

"All in the passive voice, no doubt," said Louise. "And in the plural, too?"

"With an "s," *Signora*, if I am not mistaken."

Louise stared at him, hostility pulling at her face. Zantedeschi was all smiles and apologies.

"Please, *Signora*, my father was in the diplomatic corps. We spent ten years in London, and I was at school there; a useful flanker in the school rugby team if I may say so."

Louise made a calming gesture with her hand.

"Sorry," she said.

The inspector nodded his acceptance of the apology.

"Perhaps, like you, I now see my countrymen in a different light. In fact, once you have been abroad for a long time, home is never again the place it was. You never quite fit in again, do you?"

He spoke gently and with a tone of sincerity but Ralph and Louise exchanged frowning glances.

"We haven't been back, yet," Louise said.

"Then let me advise you. Perhaps you know already, but home is where you are now. It is a state of mind. When I was in London, I did not know this. Every day, I dreamed of my country. I yearned for a bowl of good pasta. It seemed to me that everyone in Italy was singing arias from Puccini and the girls were so beautiful."

He smiled to reveal those small white teeth but his eyes held a faraway look. In the pause which followed, Ralph fingered at the letter folded in the back pocket of his trousers. The letter, which had arrived that morning, was from the London school. They had offered him the job he had interviewed for, but he had not yet replied.

"But dreams are only dreams, are they not, Mr Connor?" Zantedeschi said. "And reality can rarely match them. When I came back to Italy, I saw just the ugliness – just the nightmare."

Ralph leaned forward, his face showing real interest.

"Here in *Bellano*?"

"Let me inform you about the *Bellanese*," the inspector said. "A few generations ago, the town was dominated by farms and farm workers. Soon after the war, money came. *Signor* Merighi was typical of that generation. Their children will inherit this wealth. On the surface we look like a well-to-do and respectable middle-class society. Conformity to this respectability is a must. But let me tell you something."

He raised a finger and held it between his wide-open and dark eyes.

"Two years ago, on my initiative, we opened a child hotline. Children could contact us if they needed help. My colleagues told me I was crazy. Italians love their children, they said, you are wasting our time."

Ralph's eyes were drawn to the window. The animated conversation on the pavement suggested that the conversing group had swelled in size.

"We were shocked at the number of calls we received," Zantcdcschi said. "Nothing could disguise the fact that a considerable amount of child abuse was going on under the surface of this respectable society."

"I didn't know," Louise said.

The inspector rubbed his hands.

"Exactly," he said. "Nobody knows that between the respectable walls of *Signor* Merighi's new houses, the beatings and other forms of abuse take place and the pain and the sorrow are felt."

Ralph glanced at his watch.

"How is this going to help Nick?"

"It's not my job to help anyone," the inspector said. "It is my job to identify the perpetrators of crime and have them punished. With regard to the Merighi case, we are still documenting everything at the crime scene. As far as I can see, this is a self-solving crime but I need evidence to back up our findings."

"What exactly do you mean by self-solving crime?" Louise said. "Does it mean that you have already decided who the guilty party is?"

For a moment, the inspector looked hurt.

"We have our suspects," the inspector said. "It all looks clear cut but there are other avenues to explore."

"Such as?"

"I am not at liberty to say. What I can say is that until our investigations are complete, we need to build up a profile of Mr Radcliffe and his associates. Those include you, Mr Connor, and you, *Signora* Middleton."

Ralph stirred.

"What do you need to know? What avenues are you exploring?"

The inspector turned and shuffled over to the window.

"Do not excite yourself, Mr Connor. I'm sure you have nothing to concern yourself with."

He slid his hands into the pockets of his jeans and looked down towards the pavement.

"Who are these people making so much noise?"

"Students probably," said Louise.

"Did nobody tell them you are closed?"

Louise and Ralph exchanged glances but remained silent.

"Mr Radcliffe is a friend of yours?" Zantedeschi said.

Ralph hesitated. A burst of laughter from the pavement suggested that the group of people had grown in both number and confidence. Ralph would not describe the laughter as good laughter. Good laughter implied strong social bonds and well-being and communicated human connection. The laughter from the pavement seemed to reflect anxiety, insecurity and disconnection.

"He was a work colleague," Ralph said.

"No social engagements, then?"

"No."

"But you knew that his wife and child had left him?"

"Yes, of course."

"Do you know why they left?"

Ralph planted a pleasant expression on his face.

"We were all working hard to make the school a success. Our days started at 7.30 and ended at 10.00 in the evening. Maybe this had something to do with her dissatisfaction."

The inspector spun round and sought out Ralph's eyes with his.

"Have you never talked about it with him?"

Ralph's cheeks reddened with indignation.

"He never opened up to me about it."

"And you never went to him? Did it not occur to you that your friend needed help?"

"He could have come to me at any time."

"But not between 7.30 in the morning and 10.00 at night, am I right?"

"Are you telling me that I was at fault?"

The inspector shook his head.

"What I'm saying is unimportant, Mr Connor. What you are saying to yourself is another matter. But in my experience, men in Mr Radcliffe's situation rarely ask for help. Who wants charity? He never talked to you about his personal problems?"

"No."

"So, he never talked to you about money, love?"

"No."

"What about you, *Signora* Middleton?"

Louise shook her head. The inspector removed his hands from his pockets and placed them on his hips. He swivelled and looked through the window. Every now and then he would cock his head as if he had seen something through the fog.

"You know," he said, "we found traces of LSD in his urine."

The policeman stepped backwards and half turned to face Louise.

"Rumour has it that he often visited the bad side of town. Did he often take drugs? Did he need money to fund a drug habit?"

"Doesn't sound like the Nick I know," said Ralph.

"From what you have told me, Mr Radcliffe, you did not know him at all."

Louise bit at her bottom lip and Ralph said nothing while Zantedeschi strutted across the room and stood with his hands behind his back at the bookcase. His attempts to read the writing on the spines of books resulted in almost comical contortions of his head.

"Francesca came to see me," Ralph said. "The day before yesterday."

Zantedeschi slipped a volume from the bookcase and fingered through it.

"*Signora* Merighi, you mean?"

"That's right."

"An attractive lady," the inspector said. "Perhaps she's about to be made more attractive by a considerable inheritance. Tell me, Mr Connor, have you actually read Joseph Conrad or are these books just for show?"

Ralph was surprised by the tone of the question. It had come as an apparent afterthought while the inspector's eyes scanned the pages of the book.

"Yes, I have read Conrad. *Nostromo* is one of my favourite books."

"A very human story of resentment, corruption and destruction, if I may say so," said Zantedeschi. "Timeless themes which are as valid now as they were then, wouldn't you say? Not receiving our just deserts."

"I suppose so," said Ralph.

Zantedeschi flicked through the pages of the book he was holding but Ralph doubted that he was reading it. Eventually, the inspector said:

"So, what did *Signora* Merighi want?"

"She told me that Nick was stalking her."

"Yes, we have been informed about these allegations of stalking."

Louise shot to her feet.

"Nick is not the kind of person to do these things," she said.

"That is exactly what I am trying to establish, *Signora*," Zantedeschi said to the book in his hand. "What type of person is he? Neither of you are helping very much. Perhaps he was simply a private man. We have witnesses who say he often frequented the bars by the station. Maybe he needed sexual gratification?"

"As far as I know," Louise said, "prostitution is not against the law."

Zantedeschi closed the book and slipped it back on the shelf.

"But pimping may be," he said. "Trafficking is certainly illegal."

Ralph lowered his eyes and made a light grimace.

"There is something else I should mention while you are here," he said.

Zantedeschi fingered at his sunglasses and, pulling them off his head, he folded them and slipped them into the pocket of his shirt. He walked over to the desk and slid his buttocks onto one corner. He looked down at Ralph and raised his eyebrows.

"What would that be? A confession?"

Ralph took a deep breath and shook his head.

"Yesterday," said Ralph, directing his words at the floor, "I was attacked while on my way to meet Louise. At first, I thought they were going to strangle me to death."

"Did you not report this to the police?" Zantedeschi asked.

Ralph looked up and laughed lightly.

"It was nothing. I wasn't hurt and nothing was stolen."

"Nonetheless, how can you expect us to prevent attacks if nobody reports them? So, who were they?"

"Three men wearing Balaclavas and speaking with southern accents."

"So - as long as they wear their Balaclava helmets, we'll recognise them and arrest them?"

"It happened so quickly," Ralph said. "They just appeared from the fog."

"And is that where you got the wound on your hand and the bruise on your neck?"

"I had to defend myself."

"Of course, you did. You must have hit someone hard with a cut and bruise like that. You are a big and powerful man, Mr Connor, easily irritated if my memory serves me well. Did you knock him out?"

"I'm not..."

"I mean, you must have knocked him down."

"I can't really remember."

"Did you hit this person before or after they tried to strangle you?"

"It seems all a blur, to be honest. I must have hit out when he had his hands around my throat."

Zantedeschi slipped off the desk and glanced at his watch.

"Wait," said Ralph. "They let me go and told me to keep away from Francesca."

"Francesca? She and her money do keep raising their heads, do they not?"

"I did not know she had any money."

"And I didn't know you were having a relationship with her," said Zantedeschi.

"I wasn't."

"No? Then why would anyone warn you to keep away from her?"

"I don't know," Ralph said. "I thought it might be mistaken identity but they knew my name. They knew exactly who I was."

"Can you think of anyone who might think you were close to Francesca? Someone who might be jealous?"

Ralph shook his head.

"We were just friends – nothing more."

Zantedeschi chuckled.

"A jealous person does not believe in 'just friends,' Mr Connor. I am not sure I do, either, and I am not a jealous person. Have you ever been out together?"

"We had a drink together last summer."

"And what did you talk about?"

118

"Just this and that. It was a long time ago."

"Come on, Mr Connor, a warm summer night in *Bellano*, a bottle of wine, a beautiful heiress, you must recall what you talked about."

"We talked about the love of her life."

"Did you not think that was a bit strange?"

"Why should I?"

"You were just acquaintances and she told you about her love life?"

"Is that so strange? Sometimes it is easier to unburden yourself to a stranger than to a friend."

Zantedeschi appeared to consider this statement and then nodded.

"Perhaps you made someone jealous, Mr Connor, someone who was waiting in the wings, so to speak, and someone who did not believe in 'just friends.' There may be many of these people. An attractive woman and a woman who might be about to claim her inheritance would draw many admirers, don't you think?"

Ralph said nothing.

"Motives are of the utmost importance in solving crimes in general and in Mr Radcliffe's case in particular. We have no witnesses and we have no clear motive, you see? Apparently, *Signor* Merighi hated the English but that is not a reason to kill him, is it?"

"A lot of people hate the English," Ralph said. "Perhaps Nick really was near the house that night. It is possible that Francesca's father saw him, confronted him, and Nick killed him."

"In some kind of drug-filled rage? One problem is that Mr Radcliffe claims he cannot remember anything. His blood-soaked clothes are certainly damning but that's not enough to convict him of murder. What struck all of us was the violence of the killing. Of course, all killings are violent but *Signor* Merighi's killer went on beating him long after his actual death. His face was unrecognisable."

He made towards the office door but paused on the threshold.

"Just one more thing, Mr Connor. You have a nice car. It is a car that people notice."

"Thank you. I like it too."

"And the engine noise is so sweet, isn't it?"

"I have the engine tuned at..."

"Not a sound like any other car."

"No, I suppose not, but..."

"Where were you on the night of the crime?"

"I told you, Francesca came to see me."

"Yes, Mr Connor, we know that. We also know that you went somewhere later that evening - in your car."

Ralph hesitated.

"Don't look so perplexed, Mr Connor. Italian towns are living things. They have eyes, ears and a mouth to speak with."

Ralph turned his head away but he felt the policeman's eyes staring at him, waiting.

"I had to park the car," Ralph said. "The battery was getting low so I drove it around the town ring."

"How long were you away?"

Ralph shrugged.

"Difficult to say. Thirty minutes?"

"How long does it take to drive around the town ring? An impatient man like you at the wheel, a fast car... Ten minutes? We are not a very big town, Mr Connor. Our ring is small."

"It was foggy," Ralph said.

"Quite so. Thank you for your time," Zantedeschi said heading for the door again. He turned on the threshold.

"There are two things you should know about the police enquiry," he said. "The first is that *Signor* Merighi died intestate."

"Which means," Louise said, "the children will inherit."

"Equally, I believe," said Zantedeschi, turning to leave.

"What was the second thing we need to know?"

The inspector stepped back into the office and, taking the glasses from his shirt pocket, flipped them open and placed them on his head.

"We – the Police – have a problem with motive. Without a motive it is difficult to charge people. And if we cannot charge people, we are obliged to let them go."

"So?"

"So, you should know that we released Mr Radcliffe late last night."

# 12

The freezing fog pinched his nose and ears, and he heard it wheezing up from the lungs of passers-by. Stumbling through the streets, half-seen people gripped at coat lapels and walked with eyes cast down to the pavement. Ralph looked at them with disdain. *Even fog has a beauty*, he thought. At dawn, it left ice on the branches in the trees that lined *Via Tommaso da Modena*. They glowed like silver in the later morning light. Usually, by early afternoon, the ice melted off the trees and, much to Ralph's delight, the air was filled with sparkles. The beauty of it swept him into a world that was higher and headier than simple emotion or thought. Louise was already half-cuddled into the warmth of his shoulder. He now allowed his arm to stretch out and his hand to make contact with her back.

He lowered his arm in a wide arc when they arrived at Gloria and Gina's. Through the display windows he saw the bankers and the vendors from the market in *Piazza San Lorenzo*. They were sitting at the table near the entrance. The table was strewn with playing cards, and the animated gestures of the players suggested their active involvement in the between-hands post-mortem and banter that accompanied the game *Scopa*. But outside in the street, Ralph could not hear a word.

A jumble of his teachers disturbed the photocopying room. A lamp had been pulled down from the ceiling and it threw their shadows in shifting relief against the wall. Paul Loban and Archie faced each other across the table, and Roger Wilmot had downed his newspaper and sat like a referee between them. Dislocated, and on the periphery of the group, Ms O'Henry shuffled and shifted her weight from one foot to the other as though she were about to make her usual excuses and leave. Mrs Norton was curved over a leather-bound notebook. She lifted pencil from paper and caught Ralph's eye when she raised her head. He nodded and smiled at her before resting his hand on Louise's elbow and ushering her through the door.

Ralph had prepared himself to enter a wall of sound. He now stood on the threshold wondering if the cold or the fog had got to his eardrums and damaged his hearing. He rubbed at his ear lobes but the hiss of the *espresso* machine reassured him that his ears were working. Ralph supposed they had walked in during one of those lulls in conversations that often afflicted large gatherings. In both the photocopying room and around the main table, heads were turned, mouths were open, clenched fists hovered over tables, and glasses were held up to waiting lips. While Ralph and Louise shivered and shook away the freezing fog from their clothes, Ralph got the impression that they were the centre of attention and that everyone was smiling at them.

Gloria and Gina were sitting where he had left them the previous day – side by side with hands on knees and as still as statues. While Ralph ordered an *espresso* and a *cappuccino* and Louise claimed two places at the table, the shadows on the photocopy-room walls heaved and rose to arch over the ceiling and disappear in an instant. But the card players winked at one another, picked up their glasses and disappeared amongst the pillars and partitions to resume their game in a cubicle deep in the interior.

Louise had been twiddling with her hair ever since Zantedeschi had strutted out of Ralph's office.

"Don't get me wrong," she said to the space over her head. "I'm really delighted Nick is free."

Ralph drew the coffees across the table towards them and cocked his head. This was just a preamble to a longer soliloquy. The signs were in her unblinking eyes, the thumbs hanging in the pockets of her jeans and the way she was leaning back in her chair.

"The fact is that the Police are obliged to let an alleged offender go only if there's not enough evidence to lay charges."

Louise leaned forward, picked up her cup and sucked off the foam topping. Ralph watched her tongue slide from between her lips. Her tongue started in the corner of the mouth, licked the upper lip and then the lower, in a slow-moving and sensual action. She found Ralph's eyes with hers, and silenced any objections with a wag of her head and a raised finger to puckered lips.

"Yes, we do know Nick was found wandering around the house in a shirt soaked in the murdered man's blood, but..."

She rolled her lips across one another and her eyebrows dropped.

"It certainly doesn't prove beyond a shadow of doubt that he killed the poor man."

Louise looked down and spooned at the foam on the inside of her cup.

"Nonetheless, if the police think that the alleged offender might reoffend on release or that he might endanger the public in some way, then that's a good enough reason to keep the individual in custody."

Sliding the spoon into her mouth, Louise raised her eyes to meet Ralph's head on.

"In other words, they were not obliged to let him go. They could've found an excuse to keep Nick in custody."

"Come on, Lou, what's on your mind?"

Louise let the spoon clatter onto the saucer.

"I'd just like to know," she said, "why they let him go."

"Well, I hope he keeps his head down until it's all sorted out."

"For his sake or yours?" Louise said.

She pushed her seat onto two legs, leaned back and let her hair tumble freely over the chair back.

"No need to look so afraid," she said. "I'm just looking at the facts. You and Nick disagree about the direction of the school. If Nick takes his company courses away, big money will be wiped off our books, right?"

Louise's cheek appeared to swell. Ralph guessed she had pushed the tip of her tongue against it. The swelling shifted from top of cheek to bottom and suddenly disappeared.

"And with Nick away, you've got a free hand with Francesca. You know, Ralph, the rumour-machine has linked your name and hers like chalk and cheese."

Ralph gripped his bottom lip between his teeth, breathed slowly through his nose and closed his eyes while Louise went for the kill.

"Is it the rumours or the potential loss of income that has turned your face to white?"

Ralph opened his eyes in time to see Louise twisting her head sideways as if someone had called out to her from behind.

"The young lady's right, Raffa," Gina said from

across the table. "You're blinder than I am. Rumour has it that she's wildly in love with you."

Ralph looked up, raised his hand to his forehead and fingered his fringe.

"Nobody told me," he said.

"I'm sure she did, Raffa, but you but you just didn't see it."

"So, you're thinking..."

"I'm thinking that you see no further than the end of your nose," Gloria interrupted. "There's someone here who needs you but you don't see a thing, do you?"

Ralph looked up and scanned the place.

"Over there," said Gloria.

Ralph allowed his eyes to follow the direction of Gloria's pointing finger. At first, he saw only a tall figure with a beard standing in the street with his face at the display window. It was the absence of a hat and scarf that struck Ralph as odd but when he saw the man's face, he shrunk down on his chair. This face, this symbol of personal identity and the mirror of the self, resembled a blob of sealing wax that had flowed sideways, pulling the nose and mouth with it. Ralph supposed this blighted individual had resigned himself to a life of vagrancy and was on the lookout for handouts. Instinctively, he turned his shoulder to the window and looked for confirmation of his feelings in the eyes of Louise.

"If the wind changes, he'll stay like that," she said and she was on her feet and heading for the door before Ralph could ask her what she had seen.

Gloria was bending over him in the manner of a concerned mother and she had two coats cradled in her arms.

"If you don't follow her, you're going to lose her."

Ralph was unsure what shocked him most; the fact that Gloria was on her feet at all, her comment about losing Louise or the sight of Louise flying headlong towards another man.

"And don't forget to take her coat," she said. "And take yours, too."

Ralph shifted uncomfortably, grabbed the coats and followed Louise's path to the exit. He glimpsed his face, hard and hostile, reflectcd in thc glass door and rushed out into the street. Dropping the coats into Louise's arms, he said:

"What the fuck are you doing playing around like that, Nick?"

"Like what, Ralph?"

"Like you don't fucking know? Squashing your face against the glass is..."

Louise had thrown her coat over her shoulders and was now plucking at Ralph's arm, trying to fold his coat over it and pulling Ralph back from the brink of anger.

"We haven't got much time," she said. "And put your coat on, now."

While Ralph obeyed, Nick said:

"We need to get Francesca away from *La Casa Rossa*. She'll only come if you ask her, Ralph."

He held out a scrap of paper.

"This is the number. Ring it. Tell her you need to see her now."

Ralph stiffened. Not only were the vowels flat, word endings and intonation patterns sounded more like Yorkshire's unofficial anthem "*On Ilkla Mooar baht 'ats*," and he hardly understood a word. Seeing Ralph's confusion, Nick said:

"This isn't about you, Ralph. And it's not about me. It's about Francesca. She really loves you, you know? Get her down here – please."

The Yorkshire vowels and intonation came with a tremor of urgency that vibrated in the air between them. Ralph span away and pushed through the main door. Fumbling in his pocket for a token, he picked up the phone and poked at the dialler as though it was contaminated. He glanced at Nick and Louise. They were conversing intimately in the manner of any two lovers in the shadow of a sunlit *piazza*. Ralph slammed the phone down. There was a presence at his shoulder and a voice in the air.

"It has a smell. It has a sound - a train tumbling through the night."

The shock of seeing Gina anywhere but on the chair where she usually sat stilled him, but the touch of her hand on his arm turned him to stone.

"What is this smell, this sound?" Gina said. "It's jealousy, my young friend."

She leaned forward and whispered in his ear.

"You have nothing to fear except your own voices and your inability to see."

It might have been a cold gust of air, wandering through the door with a new customer, that made Ralph shiver, but he felt that the world as he knew it was on the point of change. He picked up the phone and dialled again. There was a click in the earpiece.

"Hello?" said Ralph.

There was another click and a voice crackled to life.

"Merighi."

While they exchanged pleasantries, Ralph was struck by the quality of Francesca's voice. Her tone was so familiar that Ralph almost saw her in front of him but it was touched by some emotion that he was unable or unwilling to identify. When there was a pause and a shuffle at the other end of the line, Ralph cupped his temple with his hand and blocked out the view of Nick and Louise from his line of sight. Focusing his eyes on the black hole of the mouthpiece, he imagined Francesca sitting at the table with crooked legs in the vestibule and said:

"I need you to come to Gloria and Gina's right away."

The ensuing silence did not have a smile in it, a bubbly feeling that suggested pleasure. This silence had a different quality, one of closing up, a preparation for confrontation or something unpleasant. Francesca's voice snapped down the line.

"What's it about, Ralph? My money?"

There was more shuffling at the other end of the line, and almost in a whisper Francesca said:

"Dad died intestate. He had no time to carry out his threat and cut Piero out of the inheritance."

Ralph looked up and focused on the street lamps. Their light was shimmering yellow on the wet pavement. And while she was telling him, in intimate tones, about her father's threats to disinherit Piero, Ralph watched the shimmering light swallow the group of market vendors making their way back to the *piazza*. He did not care about the will. He was somewhere else, somewhere in the street with Louise.

"This isn't about the money," Ralph said. "I need to see you now. It's really urgent."

From the earpiece came a harsh intake of breath followed by a few words.

"Give me forty-five minutes."

Ralph hung up after she did. In the photocopying room, his teachers were raising their glasses and a muted *hurrah* came through the closed door. Gloria and Gina were sitting on their usual chairs - statue-still and with hands on knees. Neither of them looked in his direction when he made his way through the glass doors and out into the fog.

Ralph breathed out slowly, giving himself the time to free his voice from any feelings.

"It's done," he said. "Forty-five minutes, she said."

Nick nodded.

"Then, I must go," he said. "Before I am recognised."

"Where are you going, Nick?" Louise said.

"I'm going up to the house now. If I'm not back by early evening, call the police."

"What are you going to do?" Louise asked.

"Speak to Piero. Ring his neck if necessary."

"Piero?" said Louise, "What's he done?"

Nick took four steps backwards, and each step had a word attached.

"What." Step. "Has." Step. "He." Step. "Done?"

The outline of his body smudged in the fog.

"Made poison." Step. "Caused mayhem." Step.

He took another pace backwards into his mysterious and closed world.

"Why did he tell me Francesca was falling in love with me? Why did he tell me where I would always find her in the evening? Why did he tell me Francesca wanted to see me as much as I wanted to see her?"

Nick had almost disappeared from view and out of the fog came his voice both soft and mournful:

"He told me it was her father... He hated the English for what they'd done in the war. I believed Piero. Of course, I believed him. I wanted to."

Louise stepped forward, her head turning from side to side. She leaned into the fog and said:

"Nick, Piero told Francesca that Ralph was falling in love with her too. Nick, are you there? Nick?"

"Then she really is in danger," Nick said.

"Why? Why is she in danger, Nick?"

"Because she knows."

"What does she know, Nick?"

There was silence at first and then came Nick's voice from some place far away.

"The truth. She knows the truth about her brother."

# 13

Ralph peered through the window. The fog, moving through streets and swirling round and over the buildings, was coloured a darker grey. Unnoticed, dusk had gathered and it carried with it the concern that Francesca had not yet appeared. He looked at his watch. He still expected to see a movement or a shape in the mist emerging at any time, but the streets were full of emptiness and the silence of a town sitting down to late afternoon coffee and cake.

He and Louise had been joined by some of their colleagues. Roger Wilmot was the first of the older teachers to overcome the perceived barriers of age, experience and status. Without saying a word, he slid his newspaper onto the table and buried his head in the cryptic world of his crossword puzzle.

Ralph had been watching Louise for several minutes. She was leaning back in her chair and studying the ceiling while she prepared her verdict. She shook her head and her hair tumbled down her back like a waterfall.

"It is unbelievable," she said. "The power of rumour

and hearsay – the fact that people believe it - with or without evidence."

Louise shifted her balance and the chair clattered forwards.

"Have you read *Othello*?"

"Yes, I..."

"Then you'll know," she said. "The play tells the story of a powerful general of the Venetian army, Othello, whose life and marriage are ruined by a conniving, deceitful, nasty little shit called Iago."

"Lou, please, aren't you going off..."

"There are similarities between *Othello* and this mess in *Bellano*. Piero spreads rumours, too. Iago does it to get revenge. Why does Piero do it?"

She looked at Ralph, her questioning eyes caressing his face. Before he could say a word, voices gushed out of the photocopying room. Paul Loban and Archie crashed through the doorway, temporarily united by the newspaper in front of them.

"Judas," Archie said. "Judas."

Paul swiped at the paper with the back of his hand.

Slap.

"Treacherous."

Slap.

"Bastard."

Louise leaned over, laid one hand on Ralph's forearm and whispered:

"In both *Othello* and the *Bellano* case, the villain takes isolated individuals, foreigners actually, and by rumour and insinuation, manipulates them."

Ralph looked to the floor, pretending to think, savouring the pressure of her fingers, her words warm in his ear.

"Who's been manipulated, Lou?"

"Nick, of course."

"Is Nick isolated?"

"Perhaps we foreigners are always isolated, vulnerable and open to corruption."

Louise removed her hand and searched his eyes.

"And you, despite your armour, you're also vulnerable. The power of rumour has condemned you in the same way that rumour condemned our school. And we mustn't forget Francesca. She's also been mercilessly manipulated to serve his purpose."

"Piero's purpose? What purpose?"

Louise shook her head and looked towards the ceiling for an answer.

The tapping of a walking stick heralded the presence of Mrs Norton. She was standing unnoticed like a shadow behind them.

"It's the inheritance," she said over her shoulder. "Mark my words, it's the inheritance."

The comment was intended for Miss O'Henry. She was hovering in the photocopying room and unable to decide whether to find a space at the table or make her getaway. Ralph was peering into the fog again, still hoping to see some sign of Francesca. He was casting around for reasons that might explain her non-appearance when Paul Loban's voice gate-crashed his thoughts.

"Have you seen the local paper?"

The *Gazetta di Bellano* smacked onto the table. *Signor* Merighi stared right back at him. Ralph backed away from him as if from a swinging fist.

"You see? It's all in his eyes," said Gloria. "The cruelty, the tendency to violence."

"No, I don't see," said Gina. "For those of us who are blind, it's all in the voice."

Ralph focused on the photograph of the school and the policeman guarding the front door. The article asked whether *Bellano* had fallen prey to what a local reporter described as a concentration of evil amongst some foreigners. The article pointed to the Mercer scandal and asked whether the influx of foreigners was a good thing. Did they come to contribute to society or did they come simply to enjoy a town whose antiquities were easily matched by a modern prosperity brought about by people like the murdered man himself. But what are the consequences? Drug abuse and the advent of skinheads and soccer violence were three consequences. With the murder of *Signor* Merighi, things had deteriorated still further. Perhaps, the article said, private foreign language schools should be boycotted as dens of iniquity and replaced with schools run by Italians, taught by Italians and overseen by the local authorities.

Ralph pushed the paper to one side.

"Do you suppose this reflects the mood of *Bellano*?"

"Of course, it does, dear," said Mrs Norton. "They've never forgiven us for bombing their town in the war. You can't blame them, but if we hadn't destroyed it, then *Signor* Merighi would never have had the opportunity to grow rich by reconstructing it, would he? In fact, he'd probably be alive today. A random misreading of one word so many years ago has consequences that echo down to us today."

"Don't you think that's taking things a bit far, Mrs Norton?" Paul said.

"No, dear, I don't. Merighi wouldn't have made all that money. Therefore, he'd be still alive and Nick wouldn't be in prison for his murder. Consequently, we wouldn't be sitting here."

"Are you suggesting," said Archie, "that money was the motive for the murder?"

"It usually is, dear. Didn't you know? Of course, there are other motives. Revenge is my favourite category. When I look at the world around me, I often wonder why this is classified as a crime at all. Money is also a powerful motive. After all, why work all your life when your elderly and rich relative lives just around the corner and doesn't need the money anyway? Then there is the domestic - jealousy, love and hate. What really surprises me is that murders are relatively rare."

"Where does Nick fit into this?"

"He doesn't," Mrs Norton said firmly. "As far as I can see, he has no motive. The police will probably have to let him go. If I were writing a story about this, I'd guess that the inheritance has everything to do with it. But who am I?"

"The point is," said Roger, "whether Nick is a murderer or not is irrelevant. The consequences for us are the same."

"Which means?"

"We are out of work."

Ralph looked through the window at the gathering darkness. There followed a flare-up between Paul and Archie concerning the merits of having a British Council annexe in *Piazza Cavour*. The Council was looking for local teachers to supplement their teachers contracted in London.

"Hours are better and salaries are higher," Paul said.

While Archie raised his voice, flung his arms into the air and accused Paul of disloyalty, Paul stayed cool, parrying, counter-attacking with words like "pragmatic" and "common sense." It occurred to Ralph that they were using their differences in order to connect. His entire staff consisted of people who might never have socialised with one another back home in Britain. Here in Italy, differences of class, sexuality, musical preference, teaching style or accent became the hooks on which connections were made. That connection was vital in preventing a slide into isolation, loneliness and the lack of restraint that had often led to depravity, the Mercer scandal and murder.

"Let me reassure you," Ralph lied. "We spoke with

the police inspector this morning and he told us that the school will reopen when the crisis has blown over."

"But what damage will it do to the school if one of its teachers is found to have been a murderer?" Catriona asked.

"He is not the murderer," said Mrs Norton.

"And don't forget," said Miss O'Henry, who had eventually decided to join them at the table, "you do not make your reputation. It is something that happens to you and it can be taken away at any time."

There was a murmur of approval from the other teachers.

Now was Ralph's moment.

"You will be interested to know then, that Nick was released from prison yesterday evening."

There was an audible sigh of relief from the teachers and a barrage of questions about Nick's whereabouts, about the reopening of the school, and about whether or not Nick had been declared innocent. Ralph lowered his head and held up his hands.

"Whoa," he said. "The inspector told me no more than two or three hours ago."

He glanced at Mrs Norton and raised his eyebrows.

"They had a problem with motive."

"Mark my words," Mrs Norton said, raising a finger. "It all turns on the inheritance."

Louise leaned over and whispered in Ralph's ear.

"Mrs Norton's right, you know. It's the inheritance. Merighi was probably threatening to write a will and leave everything to Francesca."

Ralph was distracted by a roar and the appearance of two spots of light that pierced the fog and swung round the road as if searching for something. There was a squealing of brakes, the sound of a purring engine and the word *Polizia*, emblazoned on the door of a jeep at Gloria and Gina's display window. The driver had parked under the street-lamp but its idling engine encouraged Ralph to believe that its presence might be only temporary. This hope was short lived. Ralph somehow knew that the vehicle had come for him.

"You can see what happened, can't you," Louise said. "In an attempt to..."

Ralph put his hand on her forearm and let it rest there while he watched the headlights dim and die, and the engine cut out. A door opened and slammed shut, and two men appeared in the corner of Ralph's eye. One of them put a foot on the jeep's fender and lit a cigarette. Both wore civilian clothes. He barely heard Louise when she said:

"And he tried to discredit Francesca in the eyes of her father by telling him…"

The front door was opening. He dared not look up. He was sure that the autopsy had thrown up irregularities. They had come for him. But when he heard the door scraping on the doormat and the feet making their way towards him, Ralph was calm, his eyesight seemed sharper and his thoughts were clear. With the clutch of Louise's hand, her fingers intertwined with his, everything was instinctive and easy.

It was Zantedeschi who marched to their table. Ralph recognized him by his designer glasses. They were still propped up on his head but, in response to the weather, they were bedded down on a branded ski hat with earflaps and a matching ski jacket. Without preamble and as though he was simply continuing their earlier conversation, he took in both Louise and Ralph with a swift and sweeping glance and said:

"Get your coats and follow me, please."

Ralph and Louise rose to their feet, turned their backs on the eyes that sought out other eyes to ask, "what is going on there?" and followed the inspector into the street. He ran his hand through the moisture that bubbled on the jeep roof, clenched his fist and brought it down with a crash, scattering the moisture in all directions. The driver responded by stamping on his cigarette and swinging into the driver's seat. Zantedeschi slammed the door and span round.

"We have been following Nick. He was here just thirty minutes ago and talked to you. Can you tell us about it?"

The walkie-talkie carried by the jeep's driver crackled into life. The driver leaned towards the open jeep-window and muttered something to Zantedeschi.

"A message from my men at the house," the inspector said. "Nick arrived a short time ago. He was met by the dogs."

Ralph nodded.

"He wants to confront Piero with his lies," Ralph said.

Zantedeschi hunched his shoulders and made a sound in the throat that sounded like an engine turning over.

"If everybody confronted an unfaithful partner in this way…."

His words hung in the spaces around them while he lifted his chin, raised his arm and wagged his finger in the air.

"But Nick is different. He is clever. He knows we are on his tail. He wants us to come up and to hear what Piero has to say for himself. But…"

Zantedeschi opened his arms wide and stood for a moment as if crucified.

"We have a problem."

A muffled question came from Ralph's shoulder.

"Which is?"

"We are the police. We can't just break in to people's houses for no reason."

"Isn't danger to life a good enough reason?"

"To Nick's life?"

"No," said Louise, "to Francesca's. Ralph asked her to join us here."

"So, where is she?

"She hasn't arrived."

Zantedeschi grabbed the walkie-talkie from the driver and spoke rapidly into it. A few seconds later the inspector turned to Louise.

"My men have not seen her and they haven't seen any vehicles leaving the house. This could be our chance."

He spoke again into the walkie-talkie and handed it back to the driver.

"So, my men will silence those dogs. We must arrive unannounced. This is our chance, the excuse we need."

"To do what?"

The inspector rounded the jeep to the passenger side and flung the door open.

"To get up there now, before it's too late. Get in."

"Why us?" Louise said.

"Just get in – now," Zantedeschi said.

He made a sharp comment to the driver and the jeep roared into life.

# 14

While the jeep slipped away and accelerated into the fog, Zantedeschi shifted his weight and twisted round to confront Ralph and Louise.

"I'm sure you know that Gloria and Gina's is the place to go for information," he said. "I was there last night. At 10 o'clock, to be exact."

The windscreen wipers juddered back and forth. The fog seemed to be thinning but was still thick enough to form water droplets on the windscreen and to conceal the tops of the buildings.

"It must have been around 10.30 when a familiar figure walked in. We almost bumped into each other. He didn't even apologise, but I expect he had other things on his mind."

He swung round and mumbled at the driver, who responded by pressing his foot down on the accelerator and flicking a switch on the dashboard. The jeep surged through the narrow and cobbled streets, its bonnet chasing the blue flashings of their emergency lamp.

"And do you know what he did next?" Zantedeschi said to the windscreen. "He sat down and had a glass of wine – all alone."

Louise's shoulder was pressed against Ralph's. In front of them, the two heads swayed to the movement of the vehicle. For several minutes, they were all silenced by the sound of the engine and the juddering wipers, and the four of them seemed to follow their own thoughts or the flashing light bouncing off the walls and tarmac around them. Zantedeschi snapped at his driver. The man leaned forward, flicked the switch and the blue light disappeared under the wheels of the jeep. The inspector turned his head over his shoulder and said:

"You really would have thought he would seek out his friends, wouldn't you? After all he has been through, he decided to stay alone."

They had left *Bellano* town centre behind them. The hills, with their high matchstick wall of winter forests, rose before them. In front of these hills, *Monte Croce* was a bald hump with a single flickering light against the sky.

"It must have been around 11 o'clock when he started talking to Gloria and Gina."

One side of the inspector's face caught the light from the dashboard while the other side of the face was as dark as the dark side of the moon. Ralph's eyes flickered sideways. Louise was turned towards him, and her head was angled in such a way that suggested she wanted to ask questions of her own.

"I left soon after," Zantedeschi said. "I can only imagine what he wanted from the two ladies. Clearly, it was not company."

They continued to ride in silence and without exchanging glances. The jeep sped through the fringes of *Bellano*, onto the lower slopes of *Monte Croce* and upwards to a crackling and starlit sky. The engine deafened them as the jeep rattled up the winding road that led to *La Casa Rossa*. When the road flattened out, the roar of the engine receded and Zantedeschi's face reappeared over the passenger seat.

"A very talented pair our Gloria and Gina. Many years ago, after the war, their services were much in demand."

Louise leaned forward and whispered into the policeman's ear. When she had finished, she fell back against the door with her arms folded and the whites of her eyes flashing.

"No, *Signora*," the inspector said, "I am not suggesting they were involved in any way with the sexual services you mention."

At a brief command from Zantedeschi, the driver bent forward and switched off the headlights. The jeep was plunged into darkness, and Ralph reached out and put his arm around Louise's shoulder as the visible world outside shrank around them. He heard the clunk when the driver changed down and the jeep slowed to a crawl.

"At that time, 1944 or 1945, many people were without papers. Documents had been lost, destroyed or stolen. People needed these documents and were prepared to pay those who could make them. Gina was one of the best."

Ralph focused on the inspector's silhouette and said:

"So, you are saying that Nick went to them for a false document of some kind."

Ralph watched the inspector's shoulders rise and fall.

"I would guess he has a plan. I would say he wants us up there. At the house."

Ralph let his eyes follow the direction of the inspector's outstretched finger and searched for *La Casa Rossa*. His eyes were adapting to the darkness but the house was still invisible. Away in the distance, *La Befana* was in her death throes and lighting up the night sky with the occasional flash and bang of a rocket.

"And when we get there, he'll show us what he knows."

Ralph pulled Louise closer. He wanted to disappear in his own thoughts but the inspector said:

"And you wanted to know why I asked you to accompany me. Quite simply, I need you to challenge me if you think it necessary. We are not playing children's games here. People might get hurt. I need to know who I am dealing with. Am I clear?"

Bumping along in the back of the jeep, Ralph accompanied his nod with the words "Of course." He scarcely noticed that at a point near the top of the hill there was a barrier across the road. They had already decelerated and were moving at walking speed when a man appeared in the starlight. They pulled up when he raised his hand. Ralph saw his shape through the glass. He caught the attention of Zantedeschi, and made a series of exaggerated body and facial contortions. The inspector said:

"If we want our visit to be a surprise, we'll have to walk from here."

He fingered his sunglasses and got out of the jeep. Louise fumbled for the door handle and pushed it open. Ralph followed her, and both emerged into a reek of explosives and a whiff of petrol. Wisps of fog scudded over the hillside and above them were innumerable stars. They could have been anywhere on the hill. But Ralph knew he and Louise had been there before. Zantedeschi was standing by the barrier from which they had watched the fireworks the previous evening.

The inspector's head was up, his shoulders were pulled back, and his hands were clasped firmly behind him. With a brief command, he called his men together. The driver and another man with a black balaclava snapped to a halt at the inspector's shoulder. Two others, dressed entirely in black, stopped a whispered conversation and turned towards the inspector. After a brief consultation, Zantedeschi broke away and, raising his head, he fixed Ralph and Louise with a long, hard stare before beckoning them over to him with an oblique movement of the head. When they were within earshot, the inspector indicated the man with the black balaclava and said:

"My man will lead us while we approach the house. We need not fear the dogs. They have been silenced – temporarily, you understand. Those two men by the other jeep have seen to that."

The two men had opened the boot of their vehicle and were removing metallic items that glinted in the starlight. Ralph watched the irregular stream of vapour coming from Louise's nose. Her face was tense, and her breathing was quick and nervous.

"Do not concern yourself, *Signora* Middleton," Zantedeschi said. "It's just a precautionary measure. The man we are dealing with is a disturbed and dangerous individual. I have to think of my men and their families."

Zantedeschi lifted his head, sniffed at the air and set off on a slow, deliberate and circular walk.

"You know," he said to the sky, "it took me time to see it, but on the night of the crime, the dogs did not make a whimper. Strange, don't you think? Those beasts barked at anything that moved. On the night of the killing, they stayed silent while *Signor* Merighi was beaten to death with an iron bar."

The inspector made a sudden and unexpected change of direction and followed the man with the black balaclava up the hill. He adjusted the glasses on his head and said:

"What does that suggest to you?"

"They were not there?" said Louise.

"Or that they knew the murderer," said Ralph.

The black balaclava turned off the tarmac and

climbed steeply up towards the house. Zantedeschi put a finger to his lips and whispered:

"Exactly. They knew the killer."

"I don't get it," Ralph said, "Nick was there. Why didn't the dogs bark at him?"

Zantedeschi raised his head.

"You have missed a most important point," he said. "On the night of the crime, we know that Nick was drinking in *Piazza Del Risorgimento*. We think his drink was spiked with some kind of hallucinatory drug – LSD probably – and he was driven out to Merighi's…"

"By whom?" Louise asked but Zantedeschi was not going to be interrupted.

"We think the actual moment of the crime was opportunistic rather than premeditated. The suspect saw a chance to incriminate Nick and to create his own alibi."

Black balaclava became agitated. He span round and made a signal with his arms that everyone should keep down. Zantedeschi made a non-committal grunt and fixed his eyes on something above them. Following the direction of his gaze, Ralph made out the shadow of the roof and a light burning in the attic window of *La Casa Rossa*.

Zantedeschi opened his mouth and closed it again. Breathing deeply through his nose, he said in a stage whisper:

"The suspect claims he was in Pasquale's all night with hundreds of his football fan cronies. He probably slipped out for an hour and slipped back after his work was done. If you have ever been in a football crowd, you would know that individual absences are rarely missed."

"So," said Louise, "you are talking about Piero?"

"He had the obvious motive. It was the inheritance, of course. *Signor* Merighi was intestate. This means that his children, Piero and Francesca, would automatically inherit everything. Francesca tells us *Signor* Merighi was threatening to make a will and write Piero out of it. By all accounts, Piero attempted to counter this threat with rumour and hearsay."

Zantedeschi got up and moved forward with the black balaclava. Ralph and Louise followed. The two men in black were nowhere to be seen, but Ralph somehow sensed their presence in the occasional squeak of leather and the smell of canvass. Soon the bay windows and the ornamental woodwork appeared in front of him.

"Rumours are quite beautiful things," Zantedeschi said. "They are easily spread in Italian culture. We thrive on them. You simply fashion your rumour and then let it fly away with the wind like a sky lantern."

The inspector raised himself to his full height. They were all on the lip of the road. A light was glowing behind the house. It reached out and covered the garden in a cool blue. Even the porch, its lantern and the wire fence were touched by the dregs of its light. The veranda door was swinging open.

"Some of these rumours founder quickly," the inspector said. "Others shine brightly for a while but burn out suddenly and without warning. But some, like Piero's, seem to catch a current and ride on it for a long time – so long that in the end, it becomes part of the natural order of things."

The man in the Balaclava was kneeling by the lip of the road, with his hand outstretched behind him like a bird with a broken wing. Zantedeschi ducked down.

"Piero spread rumours that would discredit his sister, Francesca, in the eyes of her father. It was hardly difficult for him. Francesca was already in love with Ralph. Nick was so obsessed with Francesca he believed everything Piero told him. Of course, in time, it became clear to Piero that his lies were not working. At some point the idea must have entered his head that if he was going to prevent his father from writing him out of a new will, he would have to be removed."

"So, what is Nick up to now," said Louise.

"About to show us the truth, I think."

Black balaclava slowly moved his fingers and beckoned them forward. Ralph was about to follow when there was a hand on his shoulder.

"One last word, Mr Connor."

Zantedeschi removed his glasses and placed them in the top pocket of his ski jacket.

"Your knuckle is clearly bothering you," he said. "You might want to have a doctor look at it. If left untreated, the consequences of such an injury can, in time, be quite serious."

Ralph looked up, tried to find the policeman's eyes but found only darkness.

"You know, you'll never leave *Bellano*. Go back to England if you must, but you'll find yourself drifting back here time and time again."

"You've…"

"Lost you? I don't think so. You know, Mr Connor…, or can I call you Ralph?"

"Ralph is fine."

"Good. You know, Ralph, my description of events left out details. Fortunately, the most important detail was obliterated by the beating to *Signor* Merighi's face. Piero put years of pent-up hatred into his attack. Some might say that his father asked for it. But it is not as simple as that, as you know. I hope to close the case this evening but I need you here. You make an important contribution to *Bellano*."

"Are you arresting me?"

Zantedeschi looked hurt.

"Keep calm, Ralph. That temper of yours will get you into trouble one day. In fact, I would suggest that it has already caused you considerable stress and anxiety. I am also suggesting that your services are needed here. There is nothing else at the moment."

He turned and followed the black balaclava and Louise towards the veranda. When they walked through the door and into the vestibule, the source of the glow revealed itself. The brown curtain at the end of the room had been drawn back and the glass doors were now open. Outside, three spotlights blazed down on an empty swimming pool. This image, the queerness of such blazing light on top of this hill staggered Ralph. Even more staggering was the sight of Nick and Piero sidestepping round the pool. Piero held his sister by the neck, and he was edging towards the diving boards hanging over the emptiness beneath.

# 15

Zantedeschi crouched by the crooked table, raised his arm and waggled his fingers. The two men in black responded by padding through the vestibule. They halted at the open glass door, leaving the odour of canvass and leather hanging in the air behind them. By instinct or by training, the men nestled into the shadowed folds of the brown curtains. They stood with legs apart, their feet and shoulders angled towards the three figures by the empty pool. The inspector raised a finger to his lips and indicated the rifles. The men were cradling them in the crooks of their elbows.

"They will shoot only if there is an immediate threat to others," Zantedeschi said under his breath. The look of concern on Louise's face prompted him to add, "But only on my orders."

Louise tutted, shook her head and stage-whispered:

"Evaluate the situation? When exactly does a threat become immediate?"

The inspector's reply was drowned out by a heated exchange in which Piero's fragmented English and Italian curses rose to the challenge of Nick's flat

Yorkshire.

"Why was your father so bad to you?" Nick said.

"*Cretino*, what you know?"

"I know it all, Piero. I know why your father beat you. Did you never ask yourself?"

"*Stronzo di merda*, it's no your affair. "*Catzo*, why you in my house?"

The blue light sealed off everything around it and the three brightly-lit figures could have been acting out the final scene of a stage production. For Ralph, they resembled a damsel in distress and two handsome cowboys confronting one another in the street. The protagonists were Nick and Piero and the damsel in distress was Francesca. Her retro 1960s outfit suggested that she had lost her way, ended up at the wrong studio and was struggling to free herself.

"*Vaffanculo, stronzo*. Away from my house."

"But why was he so bad to you? Why did he beat you? Why did he lock you up in the cellar? Why, Piero? Tell me why?"

Ralph did not need to pinch or shake himself back into the real world. Either Francesca's wriggling or Nick's taunts prompted Piero to swing her round. The slap of hand against cheek woke Ralph as if from a sleep. If Piero had hit her to show them what he was capable of, he had succeeded. From the corner of his eye he saw the curtain shift. With a nimble movement of the arms, the marksmen had shifted their guns to the ready position. They were now carrying their firearms with the muzzle-end up and across their bodies.

By the pool, Nick was sliding his hand into an inside top pocket.

"I have a copy of your birth certificate here," he said.

Fingers gripped at Ralph's shoulder. Glancing sideways, he watched Louise tucking a strand of hair behind her ear and nodding to him as if to say: *So that's what Gloria and Gina made for him, is it?*

With a flourish, Nick pulled out a sheet of paper and waved it over his head.

"Yes, it is yours, Piero. Come and look at it."

Holding the sheet of paper like a flag of truce, Nick took two steps forward. Piero responded by tugging at Francesca's hair and closing his hands around her neck.

"Stop - or I kill her."

Nick rocked to a halt and stood statue-still with both hands in the air and muttering, "No. no…"

He slowly bent his knees and stooped to let the sheet of paper slip from his hand to the ground.

"*Catzo*," Piero said. "Back off, *catzo*."

Piero hovered, his eyes flickering between the sheet of paper and the diving boards. There were three of them joined together by a zig-zag of steps at one end of the pool. Still holding his sister by the neck, Piero looked up at the high board, a bone-breaking distance from the bottom of the empty pool. He then lowered his gaze to focus on the paper. At first, he seemed lost or uncertain. Then he lunged.

Ralph breathed in sharply and Louise stifled a scream. Expecting to hear the snapping of a bone in Francesca's neck, Ralph opened his mouth to cry out that the neck Piero was holding belonged to a human being and not to a rag doll. But there was no crack of bone. There was not even a change in the expression of terror on Francesca's face. But the snorting-pig squeals she made were like a blow to Ralph's solar plexus.

"Read it, Piero," Nick said. "Read it. Then you'll know why he beat you. You'll know why he thought you were good-for-nothing. You will know why did not need to write a will."

In one movement, Piero knelt and scooped the paper from the ground with one hand. The other hand was still clamped around Francesca neck. Purple in the face and clutching at her mouth, she bobbed down and up with him. The marksmen pulled their rifle butts snugly into shoulders. Zantedeschi raised his hand. Ralph experienced a mental chill, a feeling of dread that he had not experienced since he watched the policemen coming up the garden path to tell him about his parents' fatal accident. Something improbable was about to become probable. He had had a lifetime to prepare for this moment but now it had arrived and all he could do was stammer.

"No, don't shoot...please...don't..."

As if in response to Ralph's distress, Piero released his grip and Francesca fell forward onto her knees while he scanned the document. Relentlessly, Nick carried on with his task.

"When your mother was alive, you were safe, weren't you, Piero? She took care of you. Now Francesca takes care of you. Now you know, don't you, Piero?"

There was no immediate reply, just a short silence in which Piero allowed the sheet of paper to slip through his fingers and fall to the ground. Louise raised her hand to shield her eyes from the light outside. It flooded into the vestibule and mutated with the brown of the room to cover them all in a sickly khaki/blue. Even the important man in the swirling cloak looked unwell. Out of the short silence came a cry. If the silence had been one of expectation, Piero's cry was nerve shattering.

"You lie."

"The certificate does not lie," Nick said.

"*Vaffanculo*. It is no true. You lie."

Zantedeschi lifted his hand and the two marksmen raised their rifles again. Piero grabbed Francesca's hair and snapped her head backwards with a violence that brought Ralph's leg forward as if he would to run and help. Forcing his sister to her feet and dragging her by the arm, Piero sidestepped round the pool. There was no sign of the damsel in distress now – at least no damsel Ralph had ever seen. The slap in the face, the choking and the tug at her neck had transformed her. There was nothing beautiful about the taut skin; nothing pretty about the bulging and terrified big brown eyes, nothing attractive about the excrement sliding down her slender leg.

"Wait, Piero, wait. This document proves…"

"It prove *niente. Catzo* – you lie."

"But the document does not lie, Piero? You are not *Signor* Merighi's son."

Piero paused at the first set of diving-board steps.

"Is no true. The document lie."

He appeared calmer now but without warning he grabbed Francesca by the hair, swung her round and shoved the side of her head into the steps. Ralph winced when he heard the sickening crack of skin against metal but it was the disinterested expression on Piero's face that made Ralph's hair stand on end. Piero was disconnected from the individual he was battering and even at a distance of twenty meters, Ralph saw that his eyes were as flat and as dead as a doll's eyes.

"I am no stupid boy," he said to Nick.

That was probably true, Ralph thought, but he was, as the inspector suggested, disturbed and capable of anything.

"Your father never wrote a will, did he, Piero?" Nick said. "Do you know what that means?"

Piero grunted something into Francesca's ear. His kicks at her shins and ankles prompted her to leap away from the blows in a sort of jig. But slowly, she placed one foot above the other and inched up the steps to the first diving board.

"He was intestate, Piero, that is what it means. Everything passes to his children. In this case, it passes to his child. You understand, don't you, Piero? You were not his child. You will receive nothing."

Piero seemed to falter. He lowered his head and wiped at his eyes and Ralph had one last hope that the polka-dot headscarf and apron, and the full skirt would break away from their captor and tap-dance along the poolside to safety. One glance at Zantedeschi and the men in black with rifles at the ready dispelled this image. They were a falling-hand away from dishing out death. What was more the blow to the head had opened a cut on Francesca's eyebrow and blood was running down her cheek and dripping onto her shoulder.

"He never wanted you to get one lira," Nick said pointing to the sheet of paper. "Why? Because you are a worthless piece of shit. He knew it. I know it. You know it, too."

There was a scream from the ladder steps. At first Ralph thought that, at last, Francesca had behaved in line with her Hollywood counterparts. His blood froze. It was Piero who had made the sound and now he was scuttling up the ladder behind his sister, as if running from a nightmare.

"All your efforts were wasted, Piero."

Piero and his sister sprawled onto the first diving platform. Piero struggled to his feet, screamed in Francesca's ear and hurled her towards the next flight of steps.

"All that time, all those lies and rumours about Francesca. What a fiasco, Piero. It didn't work, did it? No wonder *Signor* Merighi had no intention of leaving you anything. Oh, you don't mind if I don't call him your father, do you?"

Piero stood still, looking around for the edges of the blue light that exposed him. He brushed at the steps with the back of his hand as if he would flip a switch and turn the light off. Then he looked down at the bottom of the pool and Ralph imagined the thought register in those dead, doll-like eyes that only by going down and down might he disappear and escape into total darkness.

"And he never intended to leave anything to a worthless *stronzo* like you."

Piero responded by pushing and kicking Francesca and she jigged up the steps until they reached the highest platform. Francesca collapsed, slithered away from her brother but he pushed himself onto all fours and padded around his sister like a dog. When he tugged at her hair again, the inspector muttered:

"No, you don't Not with me."

He raised his arm and the rifle barrels rose with it.

"Tell me, Piero, why did you tell your sister that Ralph was in love with her? Do you want to answer or shall I answer it for you? Come on man, why did you do it? Before you go any further, why did you do it?"

"I do *niente*, nothing, nothing…"

Piero fidgeted, scratched at his head and looked towards the ground. Ralph experienced a fit of shivering. It started in his chest and reached his lower jaw and teeth. He slowly closed his eyes and heard Piero say:

"Not me…not me…not to beat me…not me…"

"And Piero, why did you tell me that Francesca was in love with me? All that work and effort went to nothing. *Signor* Merighi saw through your little games. You only had one option left to you, right?"

"No tell him… please no tell him… He put me in cellar… please no…"

"You decided to kill him, no?"

The sight of Nick standing at the bottom step brought Piero to his feet.

"I kill her… stay down…I kill her…"

He grabbed at Francesca's hair and pulled it – hard. The sight of this man holding a head in his hand was too much for Ralph. It was clearly too much for Zantedeschi. He lifted and dropped his arm in one movement. There were three thuds, in quick succession, and the lights went out.

Everyone started running.

From the darkness came a sweet voice.

"Go to sleep, go to sleepy, In the arms of your mother,
Go to sleep, lovely child,
Go to sleepy, child so lovely,

A rocket shot into the air, exploded on the night sky and danced in many colours. A silvery sparkle hit the stream that ran down to the town. A green glow shone on the roof of *La casa Rossa*. A patch of golden yellow picked out Francesca's neck and cradling arms. There was no light in her eyes because her eyes were closed. But in that brief patch of rocket light, her hair shone like a black velvet curtain over Piero's face. He was curled up and still, his head falling back and over her cradling arms.

The light crackled and died.

"Go to sleep, go to sleepy, In the arms of your mother," she sang.

And the world was plunged into darkness.

# 16

Donna slid the manuscript onto the edge of her desk and let it lie between the reject pile and the further-action pile. She leaned back in her chair, cupped her head in her hands and scrutinized the manuscript. Donna loved her job. She loved taking on new authors. They became her sons or daughters and their books were her grandbabies. She wanted nothing but the best for them and their works.

She hesitated and then reached for the letter Bella had written to her. She sliced it open.

> Kingston-upon-Thames
> February 2008
>
> Dear Ms Sands
>
> If you are reading this letter, it means that my daughter passed it on to you, on my instructions, with the resubmitted manuscript. It also means that the major players involved in the murder of *Signor*

Merighi are now dead and I want you to know why I was so reluctant to publish the novel when you first read it in 2004.

The book is based on actual events that occurred in *Bellano* in 1989. You can find accounts of the murder on the internet. However, although I have adapted the facts, much of the story is too close to reality for comfort.

The reality is that Piero Merighi was convicted of the murder of his father. Had he got away with it, Piero would have inherited half of his father's estate. He ended up with nothing. A convicted criminal is never allowed to profit from his crime even after he has paid his debts to society.

The most damning evidence against him was the fact that his beloved dogs did not bark that night. The neighbour reported hearing nothing that evening and Zantedeschi surmised that the killer was known to the dogs.

After the murder, and during the ensuing court case, Piero became quite a hero amongst the football fans. In order to impress his friends, he stood up in court and boasted about killing his father. He said his father was threatening to deprive him of his rightful inheritance. Piero added that he only wanted what was his so that he could spend the money on fast cars, good clothes and beautiful women.

The courts were lenient insofar as they heard how badly he had been treated by his father. As a witness for the defence,

Francesca reported that Piero would come to her for protection. He saw her as a mother figure and would sometimes insist that she wore their dead mother's clothes. By 2000, Piero was, more or less, a free man.

If my sources are correct, and I have no reason to doubt them, Piero is regularly seen in the fashionable bars of *Bellano*. Anyone who is anyone in the town must be seen with him so that a part of his celebrity can rub off on them. However, it may be that Piero took the blame for a murder he never committed. That evening, things did not all go Piero's way. Someone had got to the house before him.

On a lighter note, Ralph and Louise were married in the early 1990s and they were, by all accounts, very happy together. In the years after the killing, Ralph became more and more withdrawn. It was not until I met him one evening in *San Lorenzo* church that he unburdened his terrible guilt on me. The germ of the novel was born that night but Ralph swore me to secrecy while he and Louise were alive, and I agreed.

On that January evening in 1989 when Francesca came to tell him about Nick's behaviour, Ralph decided to act. He drove directly to Francesca's house. Soon after his arrival, *Signor* Merighi came back from a prayer meeting and found Ralph outside his house. Merighi told Ralph that he knew about his involvement with Francesca and warned him to keep away from his daughter. The conversation got heated and

Merighi threatened Ralph, saying he knew about his trips to the Bar Vittoria and that if he did not keep away from his daughter, he would make this public knowledge. Ralph was justifiably confused. He genuinely did not understand what Merighi was talking about. There was a struggle, Ralph got angry, hit Merighi and knocked him to the pavement. It was then that he heard a sound in the fog. Someone was approaching, and Ralph decided to run for it.

It was what happened next that was the problem for Ralph. When he ran away, Ralph told me Merighi was lying still on the ground. Piero must have arrived shortly after. At the trial, he never mentioned that his father was already unconscious. He simply admitted beating him to death with an iron bar and trying to pin the murder on Nick.

That was not enough for Ralph. He tortured himself with the idea that perhaps he had killed Merighi himself before Piero smashed his head in. Even if Merighi were alive, perhaps Piero would never have attacked him had he not found him unconscious in the first place. This would make Ralph an accessory to murder. The fact remains that Ralph felt a terrible responsibility that was a burden to him night and day. When he was beaten up the day after Merighi's death, Ralph knew Merighi had already arranged it. He told me he saw it as a sort of punishment. But it did not prepare him for the guilt that was to weigh on him. The fundamental problem remains; nobody will ever know for sure who actually killed Merighi that night.

After Piero's conviction, Ralph and Louise worked to consolidate their school despite competition from The British Council. It was Nick who eventually got a job in London but he never settled in England and accepted an appointment as Director of the Business Language Unit at The British Council in Thailand. As you know, I stayed on in *Bellano* and ran the library until my 75th birthday and left in 1995.

The strange thing is, had I stayed in *Bellano*, the novel would never have been written. When I lived in Italy, I could only think of writing a British crime story. On my return to England, I only wanted to write a story that took place in Italy. I don't regret all those years in Italy. After all, they gave me this novel. They also gave me something very precious, something that many people never even get a glimpse of – an appreciation of beauty.

Donna put the letter to one side and glanced at her watch. She had an important meeting with a publisher and she had to make a decision about this manuscript now and move on. Nobody else could tell her what to do or how to do it. Donna liked to think she was motivated and driven, not by money or by her own success, but by her authors. Their success was her success. The author of this book was ten years dead. Donna did not want to fall into the trap of loving the memories of the book and its author more than the book itself. Moreover, the death of the major players did not alter the fact that libel might be a real issue.

She got to her feet, tossed the manuscript onto the reject pile, and headed towards the door.

Printed in Great Britain
by Amazon

30694641R00098